RESTAURANT ON THE WHARF

BLUE HERON COTTAGES
BOOK FOUR

KAY CORRELL

ZURA LU PUBLISHING LLC

ABOUT THIS BOOK

What if your best friend returns to town and helps you snag a date with the guy you've had a crush on since you were sixteen? That would be fabulous. Or would it?

Tara helps her brother run their family's restaurant in Moonbeam. Not that their parents will ever let them change a single item on the menu or anything else. Her life is strikingly the same, day after day, year after year.

That is until Tara's best friend, Joey, shows up at the restaurant when he returns for their twenty-five-year high school reunion. He works on helping her snag a date with Lance, a guy she's had a crush on since she was sixteen.

Not that she'll admit she's still crushing on Lance. Not that Joey believes her protests.

Joey thinks Tara is too good for Lance. If only Tara would look at him, the way she looks at Lance…

A disastrous first date convinces Tara that Lance is out of her league. Joey wants to deck the guy. But nothing tops what happens at the actual reunion.

The book can be read as a standalone or pop back to book one, Memories of the Beach, and binge the series. From a USA Today Bestselling Author. Grab Restaurant on the Wharf and dive into this charming beach read.

Memories of the Beach
    Walks along the Shore
    Bookshop near the Coast
    Restaurant on the Wharf
    Lilacs by the Sea

Published by Zura Lu Publishing LLC

There is nothing like eating out on the wharf looking out over the harbor. Watching the boats go by. Enjoying the sunsets. Everyone should have a favorite Restaurant on the Wharf. I do. I actually have a handful of them that I love. This book is dedicated to them.

KAY'S BOOKS

Find more information on all my books at
kaycorrell.com

COMFORT CROSSING ~ THE SERIES

The Shop on Main - Book One
The Memory Box - Book Two
The Christmas Cottage - A Holiday Novella
(Book 2.5)
The Letter - Book Three
The Christmas Scarf - A Holiday Novella
(Book 3.5)
The Magnolia Cafe - Book Four
The Unexpected Wedding - Book Five

The Wedding in the Grove - (a crossover short

story between series - with Josephine and Paul from The Letter.)

LIGHTHOUSE POINT ~ THE SERIES
Wish Upon a Shell - Book One
Wedding on the Beach - Book Two
Love at the Lighthouse - Book Three
Cottage near the Point - Book Four
Return to the Island - Book Five
Bungalow by the Bay - Book Six
Christmas Comes to Lighthouse Point - Book Seven

CHARMING INN ~ Return to Lighthouse Point
One Simple Wish - Book One
Two of a Kind - Book Two
Three Little Things - Book Three
Four Short Weeks - Book Four
Five Years or So - Book Five
Six Hours Away - Book Six
Charming Christmas - Book Seven

SWEET RIVER ~ THE SERIES
A Dream to Believe in - Book One
A Memory to Cherish - Book Two

A Song to Remember - Book Three

A Time to Forgive - Book Four

A Summer of Secrets - Book Five

A Moment in the Moonlight - Book Six

MOONBEAM BAY ~ THE SERIES

The Parker Women - Book One

The Parker Cafe - Book Two

A Heather Parker Original - Book Three

The Parker Family Secret - Book Four

Grace Parker's Peach Pie - Book Five

The Perks of Being a Parker - Book Six

**BLUE HERON COTTAGES ~ THE
SERIES**

Memories of the Beach - Book One

Walks along the Shore - Book Two

Bookshop near the Coast - Book Three

Restaurant on the Wharf - Book Four

Plus more to come!

**WIND CHIME BEACH ~ A stand-alone
novel**

INDIGO BAY ~ A multi-author sweet
romance series

Sweet Days by the Bay - Kay's Complete
Collection of stories in the Indigo Bay series

Sign up for my newsletter at my website
kaycorrell.com to make sure you don't miss any
new releases or sales.

CHAPTER 1

Violet pecked away at her laptop, trying to wrestle the numbers into agreement with her budget. They weren't cooperating. How could she be so far over budget with her expenses? She was always very, *very* careful with every single expenditure.

She frowned at the screen with the Blue Heron Cottages budget and its taunting red negative numbers. Disappointment in the numbers on the screen and in herself surged through her. That couldn't be right, could it?

"Having problems, sis?"

She glanced up, annoyed at the interruption. Rob stood beside the table, staring at her with his ever-questioning eyes. Why did he always show up when she was having a problem? A problem she'd rather he not know anything about.

She ignored the question and stated the obvious. "Hey, you're back from your honeymoon."

"Yes, we're back. Got in late last night."

"Did you have a wonderful time?"

"We did, but it was great to get back home, too. Although Evelyn left early this morning to head to the cafe. She couldn't wait to check in and get back to her baking. She really loves her cafe." Rob sank onto the chair across from her. "Now, tell me what's wrong. I saw that big scowl on your face."

"It's nothing." She snapped the lid closed. No way she was admitting her problem to her big brother. She wanted him to think she was a great businesswoman. And prior to running this morning's numbers, she had just begun to believe that herself.

He snatched the laptop from her and opened it. "Ah, your budget."

"Hey, I didn't say you could look at that." She glared at him.

"Are you sure this is right?" He pored over the numbers. "It shows you're losing money."

She let out a long sigh. "Yes, that's what it says. I thought I was doing so well. But the numbers never lie, do they?"

He tapped around on the computer keys. "Sometimes they do." He spun the laptop to face her.

She stared at the screen, which now showed a respectable profit. "How'd you do that?"

"You doubled two different expense categories. See, right there." He pointed to the screen.

Relief spread through her. "Oh, that's great. I mean, it's not great that I made that mistake, but it's great I'm making a profit. I've been so careful with expenses."

"I told you that you should let me keep doing the books for you. I don't mind." Rob shook his head and gave her a patient smile. A smile that annoyed her.

"No, I want to learn how to do them myself. But I am glad you found the mistake." Two of them, actually. How could she have done that?

"We could get you set up on a better reservation system with a hotel management software. Then all this would be done for you. You wouldn't have to be manually pulling in spreadsheet numbers."

"I don't know. Techie stuff is not my forte."

"I could set it up for you and show you how to run it. And Aspen seems techie. I'm sure she'll help. She was a great hire."

He was probably right. And that annoyed her, too. He was almost always right with his suggestions. And his suggestions were many…

"I'll research some options. How about that?" He leaned over and shut the laptop. "Let me at least do that for you."

"Okay, okay." She placed her palms on the table and pushed up.

"Anything else you need me to help you with? Any repairs?"

"No, I'm good." There was that one ceiling light in the mint green cottage that flickered, and she hadn't been able to fix it. Exasperating, but not an emergency. She'd replaced the lightbulb, but that hadn't helped.

"Vi? What is it you need my help with?" He pinned her with a tell-me-now stare.

"I don't—" She sighed again. "It's a flickering light in the mint green cottage."

"Is the cottage empty now?"

"It is."

"Okay, I'll go look at it. You know, I *do* like to feel like I'm needed." He winked at her and got up from his seat.

"Oh, well, if it makes you feel needed, by all means, go look at it."

He brushed past her and out the door, calling back, "You need me. Just admit it."

She grinned at his retreating back. She'd never admit it, but she did kind of like that he was so handy at fixing things *and* at numbers, it appeared. Anyway, it was a relief to see she was making money. Not a lot, but still, she was making a profit. Hopefully, that would grow with a few weddings that were scheduled this fall and then the busy season this winter.

She glanced at her watch. Time to take over the front desk so Aspen could go to a shift at Jimmy's. That woman worked harder and longer than anyone she knew. She'd been lucky to find her. Rob was right about that. Right about something *yet again.*

Now that the numbers were sorted out, if things kept going the way they were, she'd be able to give Aspen a bonus by Christmas.

5

CHAPTER 2

Tara Bodine pushed back a lock of her unruly hair. Why couldn't she have been born with hair that could be tamed? Even a little. Like stay back in a ponytail when she pulled it back, or remain braided in one of those stylish French braids. Or even just stay out of her eyes. She didn't ask much.

She glanced across the crowded restaurant. They'd been packed with customers tonight at her father's restaurant, Jimmy's on the Wharf. Which was good, she guessed. Slow nights kind of drove her crazy. Though when they were slow, she could trade taking the night off with her brother, Walker.

They were short a worker tonight, so she

was playing busboy along with backup hostess and had even worked the bar for a bit. She hadn't been expecting this on a midweek dinner shift. Funny how nights like this would just pop up occasionally.

"Hey, can you grab table six's order for me?" Walker asked as he hurried past, his arms laden with a tray of drinks.

"Sure." Why not? She'd done about every other job possible tonight. She might as well become a food runner. After retrieving the order, she delivered it to table six, where a quartet of friends sat laughing and splitting a pitcher of their newest craft beer from a local brewery.

She vaguely remembered those days. Ones when she wasn't working almost every night. But Jimmy's was a family business, and her parents were getting older. She and Walker kept insisting their parents take some time off. Cut back on hours. Not that their father ever listened to them.

The rush of customers ebbed until late that evening. She walked into the kitchen where Walker was putting away the last of the big pots. "Aspen gone?" She glanced around.

"Yes, I sent her home a while ago. I usually like to walk her home, but I wanted to sort through the order that came in so Dad wouldn't be rushing here in the morning. I texted him that it was all dealt with."

"I bet he's still in early."

"Probably." Walker gave her a wry grin, then glanced around the room. "I think we've got it all cleaned up."

"We do. Which is good. I'm exhausted. I think we need to hire another worker or two."

"I think you're right. We need backups to our backups."

"We do." She yawned as she hung up a dish towel.

"Want a beer before calling it a night?"

"Sure." She could use a bit of wind-down before heading home.

Walker grabbed the beers, popped the tops, and handed her one. He leaned against the counter. "So, your twenty-five-year high school reunion is next weekend, isn't it? You going?"

She jumped up to sit on the counter across from him. "Me? Nah. I'm not really into that kind of thing."

"You should go," he insisted. "You'd have

fun. I bet a lot of people will come to town for it. Wouldn't you have a good time catching up with everyone?"

"I'm working next weekend."

Walker rolled his eyes. "Luckily, you know the family who owns the restaurant. You could take the weekend off."

"I don't know." She lifted her shoulders in a half shrug. How did that fit into their plans to have their parents cut back on work?

"I heard that Joey Duffy is coming back for it. A last-minute addition to the attendee list. You could still RSVP that you're going."

"He is?" Now that was one fact that might sway her. She hadn't seen Joey in over twenty years. He'd lived next door, and they were best friends growing up and through high school. Then he went off to college, his parents moved away from Moonbeam, and they'd lost contact. It would be fun to catch up with him. She hadn't had a friend she considered a *best* friend since he left.

"Yes, he is. Oh, and I heard that guy you had a crush on all through high school is coming back for the reunion, too. That Lance Richards guy."

"How are you hearing all this stuff anyway? But I didn't have a crush on him," she insisted and glared at Walker. But she kind of did. A *small* crush. But Lance had never even looked at her. He'd dated the head cheerleader, and they'd made the perfect couple.

"Whatever you say, sis." He shrugged. "I still think you should go to the reunion."

"I'll consider it."

"You are such a stick-in-the-mud. Really. When is the last time you went out with friends or had a date?"

"Stick-in-the-mud? Really? Next you'll say I'm an old fogey."

"If the shoe fits." He flashed an annoying grin at her.

"And I date." Why did she want to stomp her foot and defend herself?

"Really? Name the last time."

"It was…" When was it? It might have been that date with Johnny Smith. An insurance guy from Sarasota. And that had been… okay, she couldn't remember when that was. A long time ago. He'd been the most boring date ever, and she'd been so thankful when it was over. Although, maybe he thought she was boring, too, because he never called her again.

"See? I rest my case." Walker shook his head. "Go to the reunion. I saw on the city website there's lots going on. Bonfire on the beach on Friday night. Picnic at the town park on Saturday day with the reunion at The Cabot Hotel on Saturday night."

"I can't take the entire weekend off." She glared at him. He knew they were short workers.

"Yes, you can. I insist."

She wanted to tell him he couldn't tell her what to do, but a tiny part of her was swaying toward wanting to go to the reunion.

"I'll see if Aspen can pick up a few extra shifts, and I'll double down on getting some new workers."

"Aspen already works a ton of hours between here at Jimmy's and at Blue Heron Cottages."

"She likes working. Likes the money. And I think she likes being around me." His eyes flashed with a glint of humor.

"Of course she does, you dolt. She's nuts about you."

"I hope so. You ready to call it a night?"

Walker took a last sip of his beer and put the bottle in the recycling.

"Yep. I'm ready." She slid off the counter and recycled her bottle as Walker turned out the lights.

They locked the door behind them and headed out to their apartments. They had both originally lived in an apartment over the restaurant, but then they'd both moved to an apartment building overlooking the bay. An apartment building that was less than a mile from their parents' house. The Bodines evidently didn't wander far from home. Lived near each other, worked together.

They reached their apartment complex, and she said good night and slipped inside. Maybe she would consider going to the reunion. She would like to see Joey again. But she hated doing what Walker insisted she do. He'd give her that knowing look that she hated. Brothers could be so annoying.

CHAPTER 3

Joey Duffy pulled into the parking area at Blue Heron Cottages. He hadn't taken a vacation in more than two years and hadn't been back to Moonbeam since his parents moved away his freshman year of college. The reunion was a great excuse to vacation here, and he was curious to see what the town was like now.

Besides, he so, so needed a break. From stress. From real life. And his memories of his time in Moonbeam were days of sunshine and carefree afternoons spent with friends. He wanted that now. Needed that. Craved it.

It had been almost twenty-five years. He'd only been back once during his first year of college, and that was to pack up his things and help his parents move. They did nothing halfway and had moved to California, the opposite end of the country. Their house there never felt like home to him. He'd gone there his first summer after his freshman year of college, then stayed in Boston the rest of the summers while he was at Boston University. After he graduated, he took a job in Philadelphia. But that had all fallen apart a couple of years ago.

He shoved the memories away and looked up at the palm trees swaying in the light breeze. The gulls calling overhead. The scent of sea-fresh air surrounded him. Why had he stayed away so long?

He glanced around at the small resort. It was called Murphy's when he lived here. A rundown resort with cottages badly in need of paint and repairs. But now the cottages were freshly painted in bright colors. The courtyard had been transformed into a charming place to grab one of the chairs and relax. Flowering bushes lined the area. It was hard to believe it was the same place.

With one last look around, he headed into the office. It was empty so he tapped the bell on the reception desk. A woman hurried out from the back.

"Welcome." She slipped behind the desk.

"Hi. Joey Duffy. I have a reservation."

"Mr. Duffy. For a little over a week, right?" Her lips tipped into a welcoming smile.

"Yes, checking out a week from Monday. I'm in town for my high school reunion next weekend. Decided to make it an extended vacation."

"Oh, I think we have a few other guests coming in for that." She checked him in and handed him a key. "You're in the yellow cottage. I'm Violet. If you need anything, just ask. We're glad to have you."

"Thank you." He started to walk out of the office and turned back. "You've done a great job here. Looks really nice."

Violet beamed. "Thank you. Took a while, and I'm still working on it."

He headed out of the office and over to his car, grabbed his suitcase, and climbed onto the porch of the yellow cottage. He glanced around the courtyard again. Sucking in another deep breath of the salty air, he smiled. It was so good to be back here. He wasn't sure why he'd stayed away all these years, but the reunion was a great excuse to return. He'd briefly looked at the reunion website to see who was coming. A long list of friends from his past. He wondered how many of them still lived here and how many had fled the small town. They'd all had such big plans for life after high school.

Tara Bodine's name wasn't on the list. That was too bad. She was the one thing he missed most about Moonbeam. His best friend. The one he could talk to about anything. And yet, as often happened to childhood friends, they'd drifted apart. He wondered if she ever moved away, or if she stayed to work at Jimmy's. There was only one way to find out. He'd change clothes and head to Jimmy's for dinner.

Tara pushed out through the door of the kitchen at Jimmy's, a large tray balanced on one hip, a pitcher of tea in one hand. A stream of customers flooded into the restaurant on this busy Saturday night. She delivered the order to a six-top and poured tea for the couple at a four-top near the railing, then she swung around to see where else she was needed.

Thank goodness it wasn't actually helping in the kitchen tonight. That was not her favorite. Her cooking skills were less than marginal, even though her father repeatedly tried to teach her the recipes that Jimmy's customers preferred. She had a good head for numbers, though, and often helped with the books and inventory. She'd spruced up their website, too, and was in charge of their social media. Her father said he had no idea what to even do with social media and had no desire to find out.

Walker waved from the bar area, and she hurried over. "Hey, can you grab another keg for me? This one is almost out." He pointed to a local craft beer keg.

"Sure, I'll get it." She went and rescued another keg and rolled it out on a dolly to the bar. Walker wrestled it into place.

"Thanks." He grabbed a towel and wiped off the counter in front of him. "This seems to be the beer of choice tonight." He glanced across the restaurant. "See that guy with his back to us? By the railing. Table eight. The new waitress has his table tonight, and I think she's a bit overwhelmed. He's been waiting a bit. Why don't you go take his order?"

"Sure thing." She headed over to the table and turned to face the customer. "Hi, may I take…" She paused and a wide smile swept across her face. "Joey. Joey Duffy."

"Tara?" He jumped up and wrapped his arms around her, hugging her tightly. "It is you. This is great. I was wondering if you were still here. I was going to ask my waitress, but she seems to have disappeared on me."

"Sorry about that. She's new. But yes, I'm still here." She continued smiling at him with a cheek-splitting grin as a rush of happiness flowed through her. It hit her like a rogue wave just how much she'd missed him.

"I wasn't sure if you'd moved away."

"Nope, still here. Still working at Jimmy's." And that would never change. Some paths you were dealt in life and couldn't be veered from. She was part of a family business. And it wouldn't be so bad if she could feel like she was actually helping grow the business. But her father shot down most of her ideas. He liked things at Jimmy's to stay the same.

"It's so great to see you. You look… great."

He laughed. "It appears great is my new favorite word." His sky-blue eyes flashed with humor, and his charming smile lit up his face. How she'd missed that smile.

"Hey, you look great yourself. If you'll let me steal your favorite word for a minute." She motioned to his seat. "Sit. I'll take your order. You got our newest server tonight, and she's a bit overwhelmed."

"Can you join me?" He looked at her eagerly.

She glanced around the restaurant. "No, I don't think so. We're jammed tonight."

"Okay, maybe later then?"

"I'll see. We're pretty busy tonight. You in town for the reunion?" Of course he was. Don't state the obvious.

"I am, but decided to come in early to have a little vacation. See what Moonbeam is like now."

Walker waved to her from the bar. Again. She flashed him a just a minute sign. "Do you know what you want to order?"

"Sure do. The grouper, of course. Fried. And hushpuppies. I've been dreaming about it for years. I've already put in an order for a beer with my waitress."

"I'll make sure you get it, and one grouper dinner coming up." She turned to leave but swiveled back. "And let's see if we can make some time to see each other this week."

His eyes lit up. "I'd love that."

Joey watched Tara hurry off toward the bar and say something to Walker. Her brother looked over at him, grinned, and waved. He waved back. So both the Bodine siblings were still working at Jimmy's. Not surprising. The Bodines were a close bunch.

His flustered server brought him a beer, then disappeared again. He sat and sipped his drink. His first time drinking a beer at Jimmy's. He'd been too young before, and Mr. Bodine was strict about underage drinking. It had always been soda or sweet tea back in his high school days.

How many meals had he eaten here, either with Tara or waiting for her to finish up so they could go to the beach or hang out with friends? It was oddly familiar sitting here, yet... different.

Maybe he'd just hang out at the bar after dinner and wait for her shift to be over like old times.

She looked great. *That word again.* Her honey-brown eyes lit up when she smiled, and her hair—that she'd always complained was impossible but he loved the wildness of it—still framed her face. She did look older now, but that was expected. He looked older, too. Sometimes older than his years. The last few years had been rough and taken their toll on him. He vowed not to think about that. Not on his vacation.

But it would be great to catch up with her. Hear what she'd been up to. He wondered if she ever went to college.

"Joey Duffy. Look at you."

He turned to see Sally Bodine standing beside the table, a welcoming smile on her face. "Mrs. Bodine. It's so good to see you."

"Walker told me you were here. Wow, how long has it been?"

"About twenty-five years."

"I've missed seeing you. I swear I saw you every day when you and Tara were growing up."

"I'm sure you did. Always loved hanging out

here or at your house." She probably got tired of him always hanging around, but he'd loved going to their house. The family laugher. The teasing. The huge family meals.

"We miss having your parents as neighbors, too. How are they doing? I didn't get their annual holiday letter last Christmas."

Yes. That. He cleared his throat.

A worker hurried up to them. "Mrs. Bodine, Walker needs you."

"Ah, I have to go see what Walker needs. We'll catch up later. But I'm so glad you came in for the reunion. Tara wasn't going to go, but I think Walker convinced her to." She gave him a quick hug. "Make sure you come to Jimmy's again while you're in town. Hopefully when we're not so busy so we have a good chance to talk."

"Yes, ma'am. I will."

Tara's mother threaded her way through the tables and stopped to talk to a couple, then went and grabbed a pitcher of tea, filling their glasses before heading over to talk to Walker. He remembered that. Each Bodine jumped in to help wherever they were needed. Such a close family. He'd always been a bit jealous of Tara for having a sibling. He was an only child and envied people with brothers or sisters. If only he'd had a sibling to help him through the last few years instead of all of it landing on his shoulders.

He shook his head. Hadn't he just promised not to think about all of that while he was here in Moonbeam?

The waitress brought his food, and he abandoned his thoughts to sink himself in the sensory delight that was the grouper dinner at Jimmy's.

CHAPTER 4

Tara came out of the office at Jimmy's and found Joey sitting at the bar, chatting with Walker. "Hey, you're still here." She slipped behind the bar.

"I am. Thought I'd just hang around and wait for you to finish… if that's okay."

"Sure is."

"I've got this, sis. Why don't you call it a night here? Grab a beer with Joey."

"You sure?"

"I'm positive." He reached for a frosty beer glass and filled it. "Here, your favorite."

She walked around the bar and slipped onto the bar stool next to Joey. "To friendship. Even if it was years ago." She lifted her glass.

KAY CORRELL

"To friendship." He clinked his glass with hers.

She took a sip of the cold, golden liquid. The new craft brewery in town was making some of the best beer she'd ever had. She was glad she'd talked her father into carrying it here at Jimmy's. He liked things to stay the same. Same menu. Same familiar beers. But this choice of hers had been a hit. She set down her glass. "So, what are your plans for the week?"

"I have no idea. Haven't thought that far ahead. I just knew that I..." He paused and frowned slightly before recovering with a tiny smile. "That I needed a break. A vacation."

"Moonbeam is the perfect vacation spot. Especially this time of year. Not so hot. Rainy season over. Not so packed with tourists."

He laughed. "Yes, I remember you always loved October here. Even if you did complain that the leaves don't turn color and always wanted to see what autumn was like up north. Did you ever make it up there during the fall?"

"I did one year. Made it up to the northern Atlantic coast. Even had to buy a coat." She laughed. "But it was just beautiful. Enjoyed every minute of it. Though I'm not sure I'd like their winters. I'm kind of a warm weather girl."

"I remember. You don't even mind our ridiculously hot and humid summers."

"I'm not sure you can say they're 'ours' since you don't live here anymore," she teased him. "But I don't mind them." Though she had to admit she had grown a bit weary of them the last few years. Or maybe it was just that her life was so much the same. Day after day.

"Your mom said you weren't planning on going to the reunion, but Walker changed your mind."

"I just don't think I'm the reunion type person. But then he said you were coming, and I thought it would be great to see you."

Walker walked up, drying a glass and holding it up to the light to check it. "And I told her Lance was coming, too. Didn't she have a thing for him in high school?" He sent Joey a conspiring grin.

"I'll say." Joey threw his head back and laughed. "I swear I was afraid she was going to become a stalker. Went to all his games. Figured out where he'd be between his classes and hung out there, trying to look all nonchalant."

"I did not." She glared at both of them. Though… to be honest… Joey was kind of right. He used to tease her mercilessly about her crush on Lance. Not that Lance ever noticed her.

"So it was Lance going to the reunion, not me, that changed your mind. I'm crushed." He clutched his heart, his lips spread into a teasing grin.

"Keep this up and I'm going to change my mind back to not going."

"No, don't do that. We're going to have fun. You'll see. And we can hang out in the corner and gossip about how everyone looks now."

"So you really want to see all those people we went to high school with? Reconnect with them?" She narrowed her eyes. "Really?"

"Oh, I think it will be fun. See how some of the popular kids turned out. And if some of the nerdy kids became raging successes. You never know."

"I guess." She didn't really have anything to talk about, though. She was still doing the same thing that she'd been doing in high school. Working for her dad.

"Wonder how Lance turned out." Walker

winked, then strode away to the far end of the bar, still grinning.

"I see your brother still likes to tease you."

"He does. And it's not amusing." She reached for her beer and took another swallow. "Brothers can be a royal pain."

"I wouldn't know." Joey swiveled slightly on his stool.

"I was always jealous that you had no siblings. Loved going over to your house. There was never anyone there. No sibling to bug us." She sighed. "It was so nice."

"And I was always jealous of you. Your family was always doing something. Throwing a barbecue for no reason. Heading up the toy drive at Christmas. Big family dinners. I loved when your mom invited me to those."

"Mom adored you. I'm pretty sure she considered you a son." She grinned at Joey. "But how annoying would it have been to have *two* brothers?"

"It was fun growing up living next to you guys."

"Until you ran away from home and left me behind."

"Hey, I couldn't help it. Dad got that great job offer, and they moved."

"How are they, anyway? Still in California? Do they like it there?"

He set down his glass, a pinched expression on his face. "Ah… they are…"

"What?" She frowned.

"They… ah… they died."

"Oh, no. I'm so sorry. When?"

He stared at her hard, then looked away. She could tell he was fighting back tears.

"Joey?" she said softly.

He looked back at her, pain and sadness clinging to his features. "Mom died about a month ago, and Dad passed… two weeks ago."

"Oh, Joey. Oh, no." She reached over and took his hand. "I'm so sorry." She wanted to throw her arms around him in a hug but wasn't sure their friendship was really quite the same since so much time has passed. She couldn't imagine such a loss, and such a fresh loss at that, and now he's back in Moonbeam.

He nodded. "Yeah, well, it was expected. I mean, they were both… ill. Not doing well. But it was quite the double whammy. Even though I knew it was coming eventually, I wasn't prepared for that. Not both of them. Not so close together."

She touched his face, wishing she could erase the pain etched across his features. "I can't imagine. So close together like that."

"It was tough. It's... it's still tough."

"So you thought this trip to Moonbeam might help?"

"I needed to get away and I just couldn't think of anywhere else I wanted to go. I hated to think of being a stranger in a strange city somewhere."

"You're not a stranger here."

"Though it's not like I really belong anymore, is it? Not quite a local, not quite a tourist."

"You're my friend. You belong here." She squeezed his hand as sympathy for what he'd been through coursed through her. She couldn't imagine a world without her parents in it. They were such a central part of her life. Her rock.

He smiled gently. "You always did know what to say to cheer me up."

Walker came over. "Another round?"

"No, I think I'm finished." Joey took out his wallet.

"Absolutely not." She pushed his wallet away. "These are on me."

"Hey, do you think you could walk Tara home? I'm going to head over to see Aspen—that's my girlfriend—after we close up."

"I do not need someone to walk me home. Been walking myself home alone for years." She stared daggers at her brother.

"I'd like to walk you home. Stretch my legs a bit."

"Okay, but you don't have to." Did that sound rude? "But I'd enjoy your company," she rushed to add as she slid off her seat and grabbed his hand. She hated doing what Walker suggested, but it was a nice evening for a slow walk home. She and Joey could talk some more. And, bonus points, they'd be away from Walker and his teasing. They headed out onto the wharf and strolled along the long, planked walkway.

"Wow, so many new shops here and new restaurants. Glad to see that Sully's Gift Shop is still here. Sully still run it?"

"He does. I'm pretty sure he's ageless. And it's still very popular. We have that new home decor store." She pointed to the left. "And there's a tea and coffee shop. They carry lots of different types."

"What was in there?" He pointed to a closed-up storefront.

"Oh, a ladies' clothing store. They didn't make it. They had really trendy, expensive things. Just the wrong market here for a store like that. Even with all our tourist trade, they just couldn't make it. Barbara's Boutique downtown is still there, though."

"Oh, is Parker's still here? Tell me it is. I can't wait to get some ice cream there."

"They are. They opened a cafe that's connected to the general store now. Sea Glass Cafe. Though we all call it Parker's Cafe." She laughed. "And they do still have the best ice cream ever. They moved the ice cream counter into the cafe."

"I'm so putting that on my to-do list."

They walked a bit farther down the wharf. "And here's Brewster's. They've been here about twenty years now. Opened up right after you left. And over there is Portside Grill. Kind of upscale. It's fairly new."

"Does your dad mind all the competition?"

KAY CORRELL

"No, not really. And we have the best view of all being at the end of the wharf."

"You do have that. And great grouper." He grinned at her as they got to the end of the wharf. "So, which way?"

She tilted her head. "This way. I live in an apartment complex on the bay. Nice view. Saltwater pool. Walker lives there, too."

"So, I know he was teasing you, but you two are still close, right?"

She shrugged. "I guess so. I mean, I see him every single day. We've taken over a lot of the business side of Jimmy's. But people still love it when Dad comes out and chats with them. He's still the face of Jimmy's."

"He has no thoughts on retiring?"

"Walker and I are trying to get our folks to cut back, but it's a hard battle to win. Dad seems to pop in for a bit, even when he takes a day off."

"But he loves it there at the restaurant, doesn't he?"

"He does." She nodded.

"And do you love it too?"

"I... ah..." She shrugged. "I don't know how to answer that. I do love Jimmy's. It's such a part of my life. Grew up coming there almost every day. Sat in the office doing homework. Then worked here when I got old enough. I've just never really thought of doing something different."

"Would you like to, though?"

She frowned. "I don't know. But it's irrelevant because I won't leave. They need my help. And I'm happy working there." Usually she was, anyway. Though occasionally she dreamed of doing something different. Something that was hers. All hers.

They reached her apartment and stood outside her door.

"I guess I should go. It was a long day of traveling and I'm beat."

She nodded but didn't really want him to leave. It was nice having him back in town.

"Any chance you can sneak away for a beach day this week?" He inclined his head, hopefulness twinkling in his eyes.

"I could try." Walker would probably cover for her. "Why don't you come to Jimmy's for lunch tomorrow? Say mid-afternoon? It usually dies down a bit by then, but we have a singer coming. He's really good."

"So, you still do entertainment there? That's great. I remember hearing some great singer-songwriters there."

"There's that great again." She lightly punched his arm. "But yes, Dad loves supporting the local talent."

"Okay, I'll come by tomorrow." He turned away and headed off toward the cottages.

As he passed beneath a streetlamp, he turned and waved one last time before disappearing down the sidewalk.

Joey Duffy. He hadn't changed much. Still easy to talk to. Still asking the hard questions and expecting answers. Her heart broke over his recent loss, though. Losing two parents so close together. She didn't even think she'd be able to stand under all that pain.

She was glad he'd come to Moonbeam, and she was going to do everything to make sure he had a great time this week. A break from his sorrow. An escape. She was going to talk to Walker first thing tomorrow about taking more time off this week. She'd make it her mission to cheer Joey up.

With that plan firmly made, she slipped inside her apartment and flipped on the light.

The room was picked up and tidy, but that was more because she was rarely here than the fact she was a neat person. She took most of her meals at Jimmy's. She hadn't even put any pictures up on the walls here, yet. It didn't really feel like home to her. That was the problem. Maybe if she decorated a bit, hung some photos, made it feel more personal. Maybe that would help.

Maybe.

CHAPTER 5

Joey got up early the next day and took a long walk on the beach. He'd missed this. There was something so refreshing and restorative about a beach walk. He chuckled inwardly. Since when did he think like that? Refreshing? Restorative? Moonbeam had gotten to him already.

As he turned around and neared the cottages, an older woman waved to him as she sat on the beach.

"Morning." He nodded at her.

"Good morning. Wonderful morning for a walk, isn't it?"

"Just about perfect."

"You're the young man staying in the yellow

cottage, aren't you? I thought I saw you check in yesterday."

"I am."

She reached out a hand. "I'm Rose. I'm in the peach cottage there at the end. I came for a week's visit and then extended it. I love it here. I think Violet isn't sure I'll ever leave."

He took her weathered hand in his and shook it. "Nice to meet you, Rose. I'm Joey. Moonbeam's pretty great, isn't it?"

"It is."

"I used to live here when I was a kid." He paused as memories danced in front of him. Tara. His parents. His old house. "Haven't been back for years, but I'm here for my high school reunion next weekend. Came in a bit early to just relax."

"Oh, the reunion will be fun. I bet you'll have a great time seeing all your old friends."

"I hope so. Lots of things planned. And the actual reunion is at The Cabot Hotel. I hear it's all restored now. Looking forward to seeing it. I guess they have a big pavilion overlooking the bay now."

"They do. It's lovely. I went and checked it

all out at Violet's suggestion and had dinner there one evening. Such a lovely old hotel."

"I look forward to seeing it."

"And for the relaxing part? If you're a reader, there's a great bookstore in town. Beachside Bookshop. A great selection of books."

"I remember that shop. Used to go in often as a kid." That was a good suggestion. When was the last time he'd read a book? "Well, I guess I'll see you around the cottages this week."

She nodded. "You will. I'm always around somewhere. Visiting with Violet or out reading on my porch. Or out here watching the sunrise almost every morning."

He turned and walked back to his cottage, then planned to head out to find something to eat for breakfast. He was starving. And maybe it would be nice to walk by his old house again. He had the strongest urge to go see it. An undeniable force pulling him. Maybe not the best choice with all the memories clinging to it, but it had some kind of hold over him.

At least all this would keep him busy until he could go to Jimmy's this afternoon. He looked forward to seeing Tara again.

Rose watched as Joey headed back to his cottage. A nice young man. A sadness lingered in his eyes when he talked about living here before. Maybe he had bittersweet memories of Moonbeam.

Kind of like she did. All those yearly visits here with her Emmett. She'd thought that when Emmett insisted she still come here this year, even after he was gone, that she wouldn't be able to bear it. But she'd been wrong. It was comforting to come back to the place where they'd shared so many glorious memories.

She looked up at the bright blue sky—the exact color of Emmett's eyes. She took a deep breath of the salty air as a wave of sadness washed over her. So hard adjusting to life without her Emmett in it. To talk to. Or even just sit silently with. She wondered how long it would be before she didn't think of him almost every waking moment.

She pushed off the beach and dusted the sand off her slacks. Time to go have coffee with Violet. There was no use in sitting here feeling sorry for herself. The day was bright and beautiful. And if the last year had taught her anything, it was that each moment in life should be cherished.

She headed up the beach to the office, filled with an acceptance of her life now. Knowing that Emmett wouldn't want her to wallow in self-pity. She still had much to be thankful for. Like the happiness she'd found returning to Moonbeam.

Violet looked up as she entered the office. "Morning, Rose. Saw you coming. Just poured you a cup of coffee." She pointed to the coffeepot.

"Thank you." She picked up the mug and took a sip. "Ah, wonderful as always."

Violet came out from behind the desk. "Let's go sit outside. I can take a little break."

They headed out and settled on the porch. "I met your new guest this morning. Joey."

"Ah, yes. Yellow cottage."

Rose laughed. "Do you think of all your guests by the color of their cottage?"

Violet grinned. "Pretty much. Though not you. I just think of you as my friend now."

Rose's heart filled with happiness. "And I consider you a friend, too. Who knew what all

45

I'd find when I came back to Moonbeam expecting to find the rundown Murphy's Resort?"

"And you found Blue Heron Cottages instead."

"But you still had my beloved cottage for me. Just…" She laughed. "Just much nicer, and the roof doesn't leak."

"I hope you stay as long as you want. I love having you here."

Rose leaned back in her chair, content. She liked this life she was making here in Moonbeam. She had memories with Emmett here, but not like at home where he was in every corner of every room in her house. Out in her garden by her roses. At the grocery store in the produce aisle. At the hardware store in the paint aisle when she'd gone to get paint to repaint the front room. Brighten it. Try to make it look… different. It hadn't helped, though.

"Penny for your thoughts." Violet looked over at her.

"I was just thinking about home. About all my memories of Emmett there. They should comfort me—and they do—but in some ways they smother me. They're good memories, but they are ever-present. They remind me he's gone. I know some widows don't want anything to change. But I'm not sure what I want." She sighed. "Anyway, I was also thinking about how wonderful Moonbeam is. At this point, I can't imagine leaving."

"Then you should stay. As long as you like."

But she couldn't hide out here forever, could she? She had a home. She'd called her neighbor back home and told her she was staying in Moonbeam for a bit. The neighbor was checking on the house for her. But she had things that needed to be attended to. And yet, she had no desire to attend to them.

CHAPTER 6

J oey headed into town to grab breakfast. Dappled sunlight danced across the sidewalks as he strolled along looking at the storefronts lining Magnolia Avenue. Still some of the same familiar shops, but many new ones.

"Joey Duffy?"

He looked up to see two women approaching. Identical women. He broke into a smile. The Jenkins twins were still here.

"That is Joey. I told you, Jackie." They hurried up to him.

"Miss Jenkins and… Miss Jenkins. How are you?" They hadn't changed a bit.

"Why, we're just fine, Joey. Just fine," Jillian said.

He stared at both of them for a moment. Still so identical. Still dressed exactly alike. No, he was wrong. They didn't have on matching shoes.

"So, you're in for the reunion, I bet." Jackie bobbed her head. "Heard a lot of people are coming in for it. You had a rather large graduating class for Moonbeam, but so many of you moved away."

He thought their class was rather *small*.

"Now, Jillian. You know how young folk are. They like more excitement than Moonbeam offers."

He hadn't been called young in quite a long time. "I don't know. Moonbeam still seems pretty great to me."

"And you saw Tara last night at Jimmy's?"

He didn't know why Jillian's comment surprised him. The twins had always known what everyone was doing in town. It appeared they still did. "Yes, I went to Jimmy's. Saw Mrs. Bodine and Walker, too."

"But you and Tara were always such good friends."

"We were. And it was good to see her again."

"I hope you get lots of time to spend with her again." Jackie eyed him with a small grin on her face. "Lots of time."

Ah, let the gossip begin. "We'll see. I'm headed to Sea Glass Cafe now for breakfast."

"Oh, that's such a darling place. Donna's sister, Evelyn, is the cook. Do you remember Donna and Evelyn?"

"Of course. Does Donna still work at Parker's General Store?"

"She does. And her daughter Livy runs the cafe. They opened up the wall between the store and the cafe so it's all connected. And they still have the ice cream counter."

"With the best ice cream in the state." He grinned at them. "I sure remember that."

"Maybe you should have ice cream for breakfast." Jillian laughed. "Our mama always said never to let a chance to have dessert pass you by."

"I might just do that." He nodded to the twins. "Good to see you."

"Have a nice time while you're here." Jackie

took Jillian's arm, and they strolled down the sidewalk.

Well, that was one thing that hadn't changed in Moonbeam. The Jenkins twins.

He crossed the street and headed into Sea Glass Cafe. His choice of place to eat was rewarded when he pushed inside and the aroma of coffee and fresh bread and cinnamon surrounded him. And the exact same ice cream counter had been moved from inside Parker's to the cafe. Perfect.

A woman with a pot of coffee in one hand and a stack of menus in the other called out to him. "Grab a table anywhere. Be with you in a sec."

He took a table in the corner, facing the room. About half the tables were filled. A family of four with two little girls squirming in their seats while their mother tried to keep them occupied. A young teenage couple holding hands across the table. Two older men leaning back in their chairs, legs outstretched, sipping on coffee and playing a game of checkers.

The woman came up to him and plopped a menu on the table along with a coffee mug. "Coffee?"

"Yes, please."

"I'm Melody. Welcome to Sea Glass. We have a special spinach quiche today. And cinnamon rolls."

"I smell them." He was unable to hide from their alluring scent. He'd have to order one.

"I'll give you a minute to look over the menu."

He sipped his coffee and read through the menu. So much to choose from. He finally ordered bacon and eggs—and a cinnamon roll, of course. Then he did as Jillian suggested and finished off breakfast with an ice cream sundae. Why not? He was on vacation, right? A good time to break the rules.

Melody stopped by the table when he was finished. "Can I get you anything else?"

"No, that's it. Thank you." He paid his bill, headed outside, and stood on the sidewalk, looking left, then right. What he really wanted to do was walk past his childhood home. He'd do that first. See why it was calling to him.

He headed toward his old house, uncertain what he'd find. Had it changed? Would it still feel like home to him?

It was so familiar walking down the same

streets. Yet, different. He turned the corner and there it was. His childhood home. His heart squeezed in his chest. The old live oak tree he used to climb was still guarding the front lawn. Hibiscus plants lined the long front porch. Someone was taking much better care of them than his mother had. A porch swing still hung at the end of the porch. The house was still white, but it looked freshly painted. The salt air did a number on the paint on the houses here. His parents had always complained about that and how often they had to paint the house to keep it looking nice.

He glanced at the upper level and stared at the window of his bedroom. He'd had a huge bedroom upstairs that went from the front of the house to the back. His back window looked out over the bay. So many memories crashed over him as he stood on the sidewalk.

Coming home to a dark house, his parents often working late. How lonely his house felt compared to the Bodines' house. Reading books stretched out under the live oak.

More memories tumbled around him, ones he hadn't thought of for years. Sitting in the front swing with Tara, talking. Always talking.

Coming home after striking out with the bases loaded and losing the last baseball game of his high school career. And Tara had been waiting for him when he got home. Handed him a glass of sweet tea and pulled out a deck of cards. They'd sat on the porch playing cards for hours, chasing away the sting of his defeat.

A woman came out on the porch and smiled at him. "May I help you?"

"I, ah... sorry. I didn't mean to just stand here and stare." He shook his head. "I used to live here. Afraid the memories were getting the best of me."

"You did? When?"

"Over twenty-five years ago."

"Ah, the Duffys."

"You knew them? Us?"

"Well, no. But we still have some paperwork in the house with their name on it. The Eastons bought the house from them. And we bought from the Eastons about ten years ago. It's a lovely house."

"It is."

"Would you like to come in and see it?"

"I..." Did he? Or did he want to keep his

memories of what it looked like back when he was a kid?

She smiled at him with a knowing expression. "That's okay. Sometimes it's best to leave the past in the past."

He nodded. "But thank you for the offer. Have a nice afternoon."

He turned and fled down the street. Uncertainty filtered through him. Unsettled emotions swirled around him. Feeling like he belonged nowhere now.

And yet... he didn't belong anywhere, did he? His parents were gone. He'd only moved to California to take care of them. And California didn't feel like home to him. But he'd sold his place in Philadelphia when he realized he'd have to stay in California for quite a while.

He'd figure that all out. He could work remotely from the job he'd found in California, thank goodness. And they'd been good about giving him time off to deal with his parents. But he didn't love the job. It didn't excite him. It was just hours of working on the computer each day.

Suddenly, he wanted to be at Jimmy's. Needed to be there. Where he knew people.

Where people knew him. Anything to chase away the loneliness that engulfed him. He'd be early, but that's okay. He'd sit at the bar and wait for Tara to take a break. Just like old times.

~

Tara walked into the office at Jimmy's. "Hey, Walker, can we talk for a minute?"

"Sure, what's up?" Her brother looked up from the desk.

"You know how you say I never take much time off?"

"Yeah…" He eyed her.

"I want to take off a bunch this week. Spend it with Joey."

"Oh?" His eyebrows rose.

"Yes. I found out he lost both his parents last month."

"Oh, wow. That's rough."

"I know. I can't even imagine. I want to hang out with him. See if I can cheer him up."

"I have no problem with that. I already have your weekend shifts covered for the reunion stuff. And I hired a new, experienced server who starts today."

"Thanks. I appreciate it. Joey's coming here later this afternoon. Told him to come in after the rush and enjoy the music for a bit."

"Why don't you quit work when he comes in and sit and enjoy it with him?"

"You sure?"

"I'm sure. Aspen and I have been talking about getting away for a weekend trip sometime soon. You can pay me back then."

"Done." She nodded.

"Oh, Tara, there you are." Their mother walked into the office. "Joey is here. I gave him a table near the singer and brought him a beer. He looks... out of sorts."

"Thanks, Mom. He is sad and lost, I think. He just lost both his parents last month."

"No, really? That's terrible. No wonder he looks so sad. What a horrible thing to go through."

"Tara's going to take some time off this week. Hang out with Joey."

"That's a good plan. And let's have him over for dinner this week. How about on Thursday? We'll ask Aspen, too."

"Who's going to run the restaurant?" She looked at her mom.

"We'll have Todd manage that night. Didn't you say he's coming along nicely on his training? He's been here eight years. Done practically every job we have here. And hopefully, it won't be too busy."

"That's a good idea. I'm sure he'll do fine." Walker got up from the desk. "And I'm sure Dad will pop in and check on things after we have our dinner."

Her mom shook her head, smiling. "I'm sure he will."

"I'll go talk to Todd. Sis, you're off the clock. Go sit with Joey."

"Thanks, you guys. I really appreciate it. And I know Joey would love to have a big family dinner." She took off her apron and headed out of the office.

Joey sat alone, looking lost in thought. Watching the musician but not really seeing or hearing him. She could tell. He had that look on his face. She could read him so well. Still. After all these years. She grabbed a beer from the bar and headed over to join him.

"Hey." She slipped onto the chair beside him. "I'm off duty. Came to join you."

His eyes lit up. "Really? You're finished? I know I'm early."

"Not a problem. I decided to take some extra time off this week. You know, reunion and all that."

"That sounds great."

"Oh, and Mom wanted me to invite you over for a family dinner on Thursday. You good with that?"

"I'd love that." It was hard to miss the bubbling enthusiasm in his voice. "Wow, a Bodine family dinner again."

"You know Mom, any reason to throw a get-together. She's really happy to see you again."

"I can't wait."

"And I thought maybe we'd have a beach day tomorrow? You up for that? I could come over to the cottages and we could go to your beach there. It's such a lovely spot."

"Yes, I'm up for that. It sounds great."

"Great. There's that word again." She grinned at him.

He raised his glass, laughing. "Touché."

CHAPTER 7

Tara arrived at the cottages about ten the next morning. Joey waved to her from the steps of his cottage and jogged over to her as she unpacked her car. "What's all this?"

"Beach wagon. Small cooler with soda. Picnic lunch. Beach bag with towels, sunscreen, and a beach blanket. Oh, and grab that bag. It has a sunshade in it."

"Wow, you're pretty serious about this beach day, aren't you?" He grinned as he swung the cooler out of the car.

"I rarely get a beach day, so I don't do them halfway. The lunch is Mom's fried chicken, by the way."

"Oh, that sounds delicious. I remember her chicken. So good."

"Come on, let's roll all this stuff to the beach and stake out a spot." They headed across the courtyard and onto the beach. After spreading out the beach blanket and putting up the sunshade, she plopped down on the blanket. "Okay, let the fun begin."

He sat down beside her. "This sunshade thing is nice. Just two poles and filling up the corner pockets with sand and we have this neat little shady spot."

She leaned back on her elbows. "Yep. Pretty cool and easy to set up. See, things changed since you moved away."

"Remember when we used to come to the beach with just a towel?"

"And dry off with that sandy towel after we swam in the ocean? Trust me, this is better."

"So… race you to the water?" He eyed her, grinning.

She jumped up and slipped off her shorts and t-shirt. "Okay, but no cheating."

"I don't ever cheat," he said while he stripped off his t-shirt. Then he shoved her slightly out of the way and took off across the sand.

"Hey," she shouted as she recovered her balance and raced after him. She plunged into the water and made her way out to where he was standing, waist deep. "You cheated."

"I'm just competitive." He shrugged, his eyes sparkling.

"Yes, me, too." She jumped on his back, and he slipped underwater, coming up sputtering.

And then it was like no time had passed. The years melted away as they romped and splashed and dunked each other. Finally, exhausted, they headed back up to their spot, and she flung herself down on the blanket.

"That was fun." She leaned back on her elbows, looking at him.

He sat down beside her. "Yeah, you're pretty fun for a girl."

She slapped him lightly. "You used to always say that when we were kids."

"It's still true." His lips tilted in a lazy grin.

"I've missed you, Joey. Spending time with you. Just hanging out."

"Missed you, too. I should have come back to visit."

She nodded. "You should have. And I wish we wouldn't have lost contact over the years."

"But I'm back now." He held his hand out and she took it in hers.

"And we're going to have the best week, aren't we?"

"We are." He nodded. "And now, can we eat that fried chicken? I'm starving."

"If I remember correctly, you're always starving."

"Pretty much."

She unpacked their lunch, and they ate and laughed and talked. She couldn't remember the last time she'd had this much fun, been this relaxed. After lunch, she packed up the remains of their meal. "How about a beach walk to burn off this lunch?"

"Sounds good." He stood up and reached out a hand.

She placed her hand in his as he helped her up. She stood and looked at him for a moment before realizing her hand was still in his. She snatched it back and grabbed the beach bag. Digging into the contents, she pulled out a mesh bag. "Let's go shelling."

He laughed. "But of course. Can you walk on a beach without shelling?"

"I can't."

He shook his head. "I'm well aware of that."

They headed to the water's edge, and she paused to pick up a light purple shell, small but pretty. Joey waded out a bit to rescue a fair-sized shell with a tiny chip out of the edge. She dropped them both into her bag.

Joey picked up a shell, and she shook her head, no. He tossed it out into the water. "This one?" He held up another.

"No, see how the color is all bleached out of it?"

"This one?" He handed her a small lilac-colored shell.

"Yes, that's lovely."

They continued down the beach with her rulings on keepers or ones to be tossed back in the sea.

"Hey, you remember when we went over to Lighthouse Point and threw shells into the ocean by the lighthouse?" He leaned down and picked up a shell, then tossed it away.

"I do. Folklore has it that if you throw a shell in at Lighthouse Point and make a wish, your wish will come true. That's kind of a silly legend, isn't it?"

"Maybe." He stared out at the water.

"What did you wish for?"

"I… I don't remember," he said, then he laughed. "But you wished that Lance Richards would ask you out."

"I did not. Did I?" She frowned, not remembering.

"You did."

"Well, as you can see, that wish never came true."

"Maybe there's no truth to the legend." He shrugged.

"We should head back. You're getting a little sunburned." She tugged on his hand and they turned and walked back up the beach.

When they got back to their spot, they took everything down and packed up. But she wasn't really ready to call it a day. Maybe they could go do something after she went home and cleaned up.

"Hey, Tara?"

"Yeah?" She leaned over and picked up her towel, shoving it into her bag.

"You want to go out to eat tonight? Dinner somewhere?"

"I'd love that. Just… can we go somewhere besides Jimmy's?" She laughed as she stood up. "I eat most of my meals there. Would love a change of pace."

"Sure. How about The Cabot Hotel's restaurant? I hear they've fixed the old hotel all up. I'd love to see it before the reunion."

"They have and it's beautiful. I went to a gala there when it first opened, but I haven't been to their restaurant. That would be nice."

"Great. I could pick you up about six?"

"We could just walk."

"Okay, I'll swing by your apartment and be there at six."

"Perfect." They finished loading the beach wagon and tugged it back to her car, offloading everything into the trunk.

She slipped into her car and pulled away, glancing in her rearview mirror to see him still standing there. What a fun day. She'd really missed him, though she hadn't realized how much until he returned to town. And now they had dinner plans. She was unreasonably excited about that.

Joey climbed the stairs of the yellow cottage and sank onto a chair. He kicked off his flip-flops and brushed the sand from his feet, then stretched out his legs. He couldn't remember when he'd had such a good time. It was so nice to escape from the haunting memories of the last few months. The feeling of helplessness when he couldn't do much to ease his parents' pain. The glances they gave each other, knowing they were both nearing end of life. The look on his father's face when his mother died, unbearable pain seared across his features.

He scrubbed his hand over his face and took a deep breath. Enough of that. He came here to escape. To put those last few months, not to mention the last few years, behind him.

But today. Today had been different. Lighthearted. Easy-going. How he'd missed that. He'd never found a friend like Tara in all the years since he left. She was one of a kind.

And now here she was, dropped right back into his life. He was going to make sure that they never drifted apart again. He'd make every effort to stay in her life. Remain her friend. He was eternally grateful they'd managed to pick right back up where they left off.

He'd never met a girl—a woman now—that he could feel so comfortable with. Just be himself. And that would be a terrible friendship to waste. He regretted all the years they'd missed out on. That wasn't going to happen again.

He pushed off the chair and headed inside, eager to get cleaned up and then go have dinner with Tara. There were still so many things he wanted to talk with her about. Everything and nothing at all.

CHAPTER 8

Tara and Joey walked into the lobby of The Cabot Hotel. "So, what do you think?" Tara flung her arms wide. "It's fabulous, isn't it?"

He looked all around the lobby. "It is. Wow. Look at all they've done to it. It's the same, but all sparkly and updated."

"It's really nice now. And I heard they are doing a booming business. They're usually full. Evelyn coordinates some events here now, too. She planned the whole gala opening. It was spectacular." She grabbed his hand. "Come on, the restaurant is this way."

Joey asked for a table near the window and

he held out a chair for her. "Thanks, this is perfect." She looked out at the view as the last of the evening sunlight glittered across the bay like sparkling diamonds as she took her seat.

He sat across from her. "This is *great*."

She turned to him and smiled. "There's that word again."

"I'm going to have to work on my vocabulary." His eyes twinkled with amusement.

He ordered a bottle of champagne, then she opened the menu and scanned the items with a critical eye. She was always comparing other restaurants with Jimmy's. This was obviously a fancier place with elaborate side dishes with each entrée.

"What do you think?" He nodded toward her menu.

"I think someone did an excellent job with their menu. I can't decide what I want to order."

"I'm going with their grouper and their fresh green beans with almonds."

"You always go with grouper." She laughed. "Okay, I'm going to try the red snapper with the asparagus side. And did you see the dessert menu? I've got my heart set on that dark chocolate cake."

"Of course you do. You never could pass up chocolate anything." An easy smile played at the corners of his mouth.

"Looks like we both remember a lot about each other."

"I do. Like you like to read romance books, but not thrillers."

"Still do."

"Your favorite color is yellow and your tea has to be sweet tea. You weirdly like fried bologna sandwiches—never could understand that. And you're always annoyed at your hair, though I always think it looks great."

She stared at him for a moment. "You remember all of that?" *And he always thought her hair looked great?*

He nodded. "And more. I could go on forever."

She thought for a moment and frowned. "I don't think I remember your favorite color."

"I don't really have one."

"That makes me feel better. I do know you like those thriller books that I could never get into. Evelyn's husband, Rob Bentley, writes thrillers. I read one and it was really good, but just not my kind of book."

"I'll have to try one of his."

"I do remember more about you, though. You're a morning person. Your favorite dessert is apple pie. You hate bologna." She grinned. "A shortcoming, but I still like you."

"You know, we should try another restaurant tomorrow. You could scope out all the competition."

"We should." She nodded, wondering if she could take another night off from work, but it did sound like fun. She could count it as research toward dragging Jimmy's into the modern age. Not that her father would let her change anything. It had been a six-month fight to get him to agree to the new craft beer.

Their champagne arrived, and the waiter poured them both a glass, then set it in an ice bucket to stay chilled.

Joey raised his glass. "To our friendship. May it never waver again."

She liked that toast. Loved that they'd fallen right back into their easy friendship. She raised her glass. "To us. And to you not running away from home again and leaving me behind."

"Ouch." He laughed. "We'll try harder this time to keep in touch."

"We will."

"Looks like I'm interrupting a celebration."

She froze, recognizing that voice even after all these years. She looked up and stared, her mouth dropping open. Lance Richards stood right beside the table. Her breath caught and her heart did a little flip. He was strikingly handsome, even more so than high school days. A touch of gray at his temples only made him more good-looking. His boyish smile she remembered so well. Perfect tan. Dressed impeccably in khaki slacks with a crisp crease and not one wrinkle. A light blue button-down shirt with the sleeves neatly rolled up a few times. A deliberate casual that wasn't *quite* casual.

Quick check—no wedding ring. Not that it mattered, right? Why was she even checking?

"Lance, good to see you." Joey filled in the silence.

"Hey, Duffy." Lance nodded briefly, then turned to her. "Wow, Tara. You've turned into quite a looker. Good to see you."

She soaked up the glance of approval in his eyes.

Talk. Get your words out. *A looker.* He thought she was a looker? That meant he thought she was pretty, right? "Hi, Lance." Two words were all she could manage.

"I was having dinner with my folks." He pointed across the room to a large table full of well-dressed people. "But I saw Tara and just had to come over and say hi."

She glanced at Joey and couldn't quite read his face. Was he annoyed? Amused? She turned to Lance. "Glad you came over. I hear quite a few people are coming to town for our reunion."

"I had to be in town on business to help Dad close a deal. Just happened to be the week of the reunion." Lance shrugged his broad shoulders. "Otherwise I'd never have come in for it. But as long as I'm here, I figured I'd go."

"I'm sure it will be fun." That was weak, wasn't it? Did she sound like a simpleton?

"So, you two. You were always pals, weren't you?"

"We were. We *are*." Joey set down his champagne glass, then picked it up again, took a sip, and set it right back down.

"Just pals, though. Right? So you wouldn't mind if I ask Tara out to dinner for tomorrow?"

"Don't ask me for permission, ask Tara." Joey leaned forward and fiddled with his silverware.

"Tara, dinner tomorrow?"

And there it was. After all these years. Lance Richards had noticed her and asked her out. She looked over at Joey. "Joey and I were talking about going out to dinner."

Joey shrugged. "Nah, go ahead. We can scout out restaurants some other time."

"Then I'd... I'd love to." Though a flash of guilt jabbed her at accepting Lance's invite and postponing Joey's.

"Great. Mother said there's finally a nice restaurant on the wharf. Portside Grill. Could you meet me there at seven? I have a cocktail charity thing going on before that."

"Sure." A date with Lance. A date with Lance. It kept running through her mind as she sat there grinning like a fool.

"I'll see you then." Lance smiled at her, ignored Joey, turned away, and strode across the room toward his parents' table with long, confident strides.

"There's finally a nice restaurant on the wharf?" Joey raised an eyebrow. "Jimmy's is a nice restaurant."

"Oh, you know what he meant. Fancier." She tore her gaze from Lance and back to Joey.

"You finally got your wish. A date with Lance."

"You think it's really a date? More like just catching up, right?" But it was a date, wasn't it?

"It's a date." Joey shook his head. "You got your date with Lance."

"I... can't believe it." She grabbed her champagne and took a sip, her heart pounding riotously in her chest. Lance Richards had asked her out. *Her.*

Joey took his champagne and sipped it, staring over at Tara, who kept glancing over toward Lance's table. Her eyes sparkled with excitement. She'd finally gotten what she wanted. A date with Lance. He should be happy for his friend, right? She'd finally gotten her wish after all these years.

But the guy rubbed him wrong. He always

had. He was so full of himself. So self-absorbed. He never could understand what Tara saw in Lance.

And he'd been having the best time tonight with Tara. Now she was all distracted, wrapped up in her good fortune about her date.

"So, pretty cool, huh? A date with Lance." He pasted on a smile and attempted to sound happy for her.

She turned from staring across the room at Lance and looked at him, her eyes filled with delight. "I can't believe it. Lance Richards asked me out."

"I'm sure you'll have a great time." Though as soon as he said it, his stomach clenched. He didn't want her to have a great time. He wanted her to see Lance as he really was. A conceited, full-of-himself jerk. Surely now that she was an adult, not a starry-eyed teenager, she'd see that. Wouldn't she?

Or would she?

The server brought their meals, and they chatted while they ate, but the easy camaraderie was broken. She spent half the meal watching Lance, preoccupied. But then, why not? She'd had the biggest crush ever on Lance when they were younger. Why wouldn't she be excited that he'd asked her out now? Finally, after all these years. Of course, she was happy.

And he should feel happy for her. He should. She was his friend. There was some kind of unwritten rule of friendship that you were happy for your friend when something good happened to them. He was certain that rule existed. So he was happy for her.

If he kept saying it enough, maybe he'd believe it.

Lance and his party finally left as the chocolate dessert was delivered to their table. Maybe now she'd relax and quit staring across the room.

She dug her fork into the cake and took a bite. "Oh, this is so delicious." Her face lit up. "Take a bite." She motioned to the cake.

He picked up his fork and took a small bite. He liked chocolate, but it wasn't his first choice of dessert. "It's good."

"No, it's *great*." She grinned at him.

"I see I'm a good influence on you. You're catching my affinity for the word great." And with Lance gone, they fell back into their easy conversation, thank goodness. Maybe the guy could get called out of town before the reunion. That would make it a much better weekend. *Much* better.

Though not for Tara. She was happy that Lance had asked her out. And he was happy for her. Really, he was. *He was.*

CHAPTER 9

The next afternoon Evelyn paused and put down the dish she was holding as she felt a kiss on her neck. "You better be careful that my husband doesn't see you kissing me."

She turned around and snuggled into Rob's arms, more than happy to take a quick break from working to enjoy her new husband's presence.

"So that husband of yours is the jealous type?"

"I'm not sure. I don't think he'll ever have a reason to be jealous." She leaned back to gaze into his eyes.

"That's a good thing. Have I ever told you that you're my favorite wife?"

"So, you've had many?" she teased.

"Well, no. Just you. But you're still my favorite." He lightly kissed her forehead.

"You just say that because you heard there was pecan pie today here at the cafe."

"I might have run into the Jenkins twins, who *might* have mentioned that."

She pulled out of his arms. "Here, let me get you a slice with some whipped cream."

"I won't say no to that."

She got him the pie, and he perched on a stool while she gathered ingredients to make crusts for pot pies for dinner this evening.

"You sure you're not working too hard?"

"Why does everyone keep asking me that?" She shook her head.

"Because you were in a horrible accident. And I thought I might lose you," he said softly. "I just want to make sure you're okay. You're safe."

She turned and kissed him gently. "I'm fine. Really. And I love being here in the kitchen."

"I know you do. Trying new recipes. Trying to outdo yourself each time." He laughed. "Just don't overdo it."

"I won't."

Melody came walking into the kitchen. "Oh, hey, Rob. Didn't know you were here. But then, Evelyn did make pecan pie."

"Hey, does everyone know my weakness for pecan pie?"

"That, and peach pie." Evelyn loved baking for Rob, making his favorite, and his enthusiasm for her cooking.

"And a nice big ice cream sundae with Evelyn's special chocolate sauce," Melody added.

"Okay, okay. I love everything Evelyn makes. There, I've confessed." His eyes shone as he smiled at her.

"I just came in to get a piece of pie for Ethan."

"Oh, Ethan's here?" Evelyn smothered a smile, but Rob caught on and grinned.

"Uh-huh." Melody grabbed a piece of pie, smothered it with whipped cream, and left to go deliver it to Ethan.

"He's in here every day, isn't he?" Rob asked.

"At least once, if not twice."

"And Melody still has not a clue that he likes her?"

"Nope, not a clue." She sighed. "I've tried to nudge her a bit, but I'm having no success. Ethan is a nice guy. Just shy. I hope he finally works up his nerve to ask her out."

"He'll ask her out on his own timeline."

She nodded. "So, how's Violet? I have to run over and see her. I haven't seen her since we got back from our honeymoon."

"She's fine. Stubborn as ever. I know I could help with some repairs at the cottages, but she won't let me. She wants to do it alone." He let out a long sigh.

"I think you should let her, then. She'll ask if she really needs help. She needs to feel like it's all hers, you know? Like she can make it all on her own."

"You're right, but it's hard when I know I can help."

"You're a wonderful brother, but you do need to let her spread her wings and fly."

He laughed. "That's very hard for me. I always feel like I need to protect her."

Evelyn leaned over and kissed him. "I'm pretty sure Violet is one of the strongest women I know. She doesn't need her big brother protecting her. She needs his support."

He sighed again. "And you're right, as usual."

She flashed him a grin. "I am right, aren't I?"

He slipped off the stool and pulled her into his arms. Flour handprints appeared on his shirt where she rested her hands, but he didn't seem to care. "And I was right to marry you. You're the best thing to ever happen to me."

He kissed her again, a long, lingering kiss. And she had to agree with him. Marrying her was the best thing ever... because she couldn't be happier or more content.

CHAPTER 10

Tara walked into the office at Jimmy's. "Hey, Walker. I have another favor to ask."

He looked up from the desk. "Sure, shoot."

"I need tonight off."

"You and Joey doing something again?"

"Ah… no. I have a date."

His eyes widened. "A date? My little sis has a date? Who with?"

"Uh… Lance."

He threw back his head and laughed. "You finally got your date with Lance Richards? Perfect. Now maybe you can quit mooning after him like a lovesick puppy."

"I do not."

Aspen appeared at the doorway. "Hey, what's going on? I heard Walker laughing all the way out in the hallway."

"My sister has a date with Lance Richards. She's had a crush on him since she's been about, I don't know, ten?"

"I have not." She glared at him.

"Well, I think that's nice. A date with someone you've liked for a while." Aspen stepped into the room. "Where are you going?"

"Portside Grill."

"Ah, traitor. Going to our competitor on the wharf," Walker teased.

"Come on, Walker. Give me a break." She shook her head. "So you can get my shift covered tonight?"

"Sure thing. You go out on your dream date." He flashed an annoying grin at her.

"You're impossible." She turned and stalked out of the office.

By late afternoon, she'd had enough of Walker's relentless teasing every time he saw her. "I'm headed home." She took off her server apron and stuffed it into his hands.

Walker took the apron, then his face grew

RESTAURANT ON THE WHARF

serious. "I do hope you have a good time tonight, sis. I do."

"Thanks." Too bad his attitude hadn't changed until late afternoon. She knew he really did have her best interests at heart. He just loved teasing her.

She hurried home and took a shower. After a full hour of wrestling with her hair to try to make it look presentable, she headed toward her closet. It was mostly filled with clothes suitable for work. She didn't have a lot of opportunities to wear much else. She sorted through the few dresses she had. Too fancy. Too bland. Too red and an ugly brick-red shade... what had she been thinking? Then finally she pulled out a pale mint-green dress. She shrugged into it and walked over to the full-length mirror. She'd always loved this dress, though it was about ten years old by now. Did it look like it? She turned this way and that, checking it out.

It would have to work because she really had no time to find something else. She chose a silver necklace and bracelet to go with it. Then she dug through her shoes until she came up with some strappy sandals that would have to work. Too bad she wasn't a heels person. He was probably used to dating women who could balance on those impossibly spiky things.

She'd given herself plenty of time to walk to the wharf. Lance would probably drive and most likely drive her home afterward. She glanced around the apartment, wishing it looked nicer or she'd managed to put up anything on the walls. Adjusting the pillows on the couch and straightening a stack of magazines on the coffee table was the best she could do. But just in case he wanted to come in, she wanted the apartment presentable.

She headed out of her apartment and down the street. She had plenty of time. With each step, her mind sang out, a date with Lance. She was too old for this teenage excitement about a date. Yet, here she was. Excited. Happy. Nervous. Her pulse raced through her veins and her heart beat double time as if she'd just run a mile.

There was no denying it. She was positively thrilled to be going on a date with Lance.

She walked into Portside Grill and looked around the waiting area. No Lance. She looked at her watch. She was a little early. She walked up to the hostess station.

"May I help you?"

"I'm meeting someone. Lance Richards."

"Yes, we have a reservation. Would you like to be seated and wait for him there?"

"Yes, please." Better than standing here waiting.

She followed the hostess to a table near the window and took a seat. The inside of the restaurant was precisely done in rich tones. No real seaside vibe, but definitely a stylish, opulent vibe. A pang of guilt flashed through her. But the view here wasn't nearly as nice as at Jimmy's. She quickly defended her restaurant.

Here, channel markers split through the water, guiding boats into a nearby canal. A pelican perched on top of a marker. There should be some view of the sunset here, but not like at Jimmy's, where the view of the whole bay exploded with the colors of the sunset.

A server came over. "Could I get you a drink while you wait?"

Should she? What if he wanted to order a fancy bottle of wine or something? But she couldn't just sit here. "Ah, yes. A glass of pinot grigio, please."

He returned with the wine, and she took a sip.

Crisp, cool. Very tasty. She leaned back in her chair and looked around the room. The restaurant was full of customers, even on this midweek evening. People were dressed in fancy outfits. Many of the men were in business shirts and even some ties. Not the usual attire for southern Florida. She glanced down at her simple dress, hoping she fit in.

She nursed the wine for twenty minutes, trying not to look at her watch every single minute. He did say he had a cocktail affair to go to first. He was probably just running a bit late from that.

After another twenty minutes, she noticed people glancing her way with questioning looks. Or maybe she was imagining that. She shifted uncomfortably in her seat and dug her phone out of her purse to make sure she hadn't missed a call. But then, he didn't have her number, did he? He could have called the restaurant to let her know he was going to be late, though.

She stopped the server when he walked past. "Could you check and see if there's a message for me? Tara Bodine."

"Yes, ma'am." Was that a look of knowing pity he gave her?

He came back in a few minutes. "No message. Would you care for another drink or maybe order an appetizer while you wait?"

"No, I'm fine." The heat of a blush crept across her cheeks. Lance was fifty minutes late now, but who's counting? Well, she was. *Fifty minutes.*

Just then the Jenkins twins walked toward her table. Great, just great.

"Tara, surprised to see you here." Jillian arched her eyebrows and pursed her lips.

"I'm meeting Lance Richards. I went to high school with him."

Jillian frowned slightly. "Oh, I remember him. Sports guy, right?"

"That's right."

"You remember, Jillian. His father is the CEO of that big bank in Sarasota. They run with the country club crowd. Mrs. Richards always acts like she doesn't know us even though she's met us many, many times." Jackie's forehead furrowed with disapproval.

"I'm sorry." What did a person say to that? But the twins were right. The Richards were known for being pretty stuffy. Though that was kind of a mean thing to think about Lance's parents, wasn't it?

"I guess he's in for the big reunion?"

"Yes, and business with his father."

"Well, I hope you have a nice evening." Jackie took her sister's arm, and they headed to their table.

Lance better show up soon, or the twins would be talking to everyone about how he'd stood her up. She glanced at her watch again. An hour. He was one hour late. Suddenly, she was over it. And over all the looks aimed at her as she sat here alone, waiting.

She waved to the waiter. "I'll just have the check for my drink." She tried to ignore the pitying look she got. That time, she couldn't deny it.

She dropped cash on the table and left the restaurant only to stand in the middle of the wharf. Now what? If she headed to Jimmy's, Walker would be full of questions. But really, where else did she have to go? Go home alone to her apartment and wonder why Lance stood her up? All the prior excitement for the evening disappeared in a poof of broken dreams. She was a fool.

One last glance toward the entrance to the wharf—no Lance. No doubt the twins saw her leave and her now empty table. She'd be the talk of the town tomorrow. Just great. Her heart plunged as she slowly trudged to Jimmy's.

CHAPTER 11

She reached Jimmy's, took a deep breath to steady herself, and headed inside. "Hey, you look nice," Aspen greeted her as she walked in. "I heard you had a date."

"Yeah, well, it didn't happen." She stalked past Aspen, then stopped and turned back. "Sorry, didn't mean to be rude."

"No, that's okay." Was that a look of pity on Aspen's face? She was so over pitying looks.

"Lance never showed up." She tried to look nonchalant.

"I'm sorry."

She shrugged. "Must have gotten our wires crossed or something."

She pushed through the door to the outside

seating and saw Joey sitting at the bar, chatting with Walker and sipping a beer. Great, now she would have to deal with both of them.

She walked over and plopped her purse on the bar, slipping onto the stool beside Joey. "Walker, give me a beer."

"Hey, what are you doing here? That's the shortest date on record."

She carefully hid her disappointment and squared her shoulders. "Lance never showed."

"He didn't?" Joey's eyes narrowed.

"Maybe we got our signals crossed."

"Tara, I was there last night when he asked you. He said he'd meet you at Portside Grill at seven. How long did you wait for him?"

She looked down at her watch as if she didn't know exactly how long she waited, then looked back up. "I waited an hour."

"The guy's an idiot." Joey scowled.

"A real jerk," Walker added. "Sorry, sis."

"Oh, it's not a big deal." But it kind of was. She felt like a fool. All those years of wondering what it would be like to date Lance. And then... he'd asked her out. All that anticipation. The decisions on what to wear. Fighting with her hair. How nervous she'd been.

All that for nothing. Nothing at all.

She reached for her beer and took a long swallow, then turned to Joey and Walker. "And wipe those pitying looks off your faces. I'm a big girl. I can deal with being stood up."

"His loss, Tara. His loss." Joey's eyes shone with sympathy she didn't want.

"I'm fine. Really. Let's talk about something else."

"Sure." Walker paused. "The new server I hired is a gem. Knows his stuff. Already handling a full load of tables. I told you I'm the best at hiring." Walker filled a bowl of nuts and slid them across to her. "Have you eaten?"

"Nah, just had a drink while I waited." And waited. And waited. While people stared at her sitting there all alone. Obviously waiting for someone. Who obviously wasn't showing up. Anger bubbled below the surface, intertwined with her embarrassment.

"I'm starving. Let's order," Joey offered. "Eat here at the bar. How about that?"

"Sure, why not?" She nodded. Joey was always there for her when she needed him. Well, he used to be, and he was now that he was back in town.

~

Anger surged through Joey. How dare Lance stand her up? What a lousy thing to do. His opinion of the guy sank even lower, if that were even possible. The look on Tara's face—which she was trying so hard to hide—made his heart squeeze in his chest. He couldn't bear to see her hurt.

She looked at him, then Walker. "Quit looking at me like that. And really, can we just not talk about it?"

She made a valiant effort to look like she was just fine. But she wasn't. He knew her well enough to know that.

"You've got it. No talking about… it." He nodded, willing to give her space.

They ordered their meal, then sat sipping their beers, giving her time to make peace with her evening.

Then, to his utter dismay, Lance walked up to the bar.

"Ah, Tara, there you are. I got tied up with the charity event my mother was throwing. You know how it is. I went to Portside Grill, but you were gone."

Joey stared at Lance in disbelief. She left after waiting *over an hour*, you jerk. He barely kept the words to himself. "And you lost your phone? Couldn't call and say you were tied up?" Joey couldn't help himself. Those words slipped out.

"I didn't want to be rude and be on my phone at the event." Lance flashed a coaxing smile at Tara. "Don't be mad."

But rude enough not to let Tara know he was late… or not coming at all.

"I'm not mad," she answered quickly. Too quickly.

He could tell she was mad. And hurt. He wanted to lean over and wipe that smile off Lance's face.

"We should try again tomorrow. How about it? I promise nothing will stop me this time."

Say no. He stared at Tara. She wouldn't give this guy another chance, would she?

"I'm not sure… I might be working."

Walker stood silent, not contradicting her, though Joey knew Tara wasn't working tomorrow night.

"Oh, come on. Your family owns the place. You can take the night off, right, Walker?"

"It's up to Tara." Walker's face froze in a stony look, barely disguising his anger.

Tara stared at Lance for a few moments, and Joey knew the very second she decided to say yes. He balled his fists, waiting for the words he knew were coming.

"Sure, that would work." Tara nodded.

"Great. How about I pick you up and take you to the country club? Mother and Father are hosting a dinner. I'm sure they'd love for you to come, too."

"The country club with your parents?" Panic hovered in her eyes. "Oh... I..." Tara swiveled to look at him as if asking him to rescue her. But she was a grown woman. She'd said yes. Made her own choices. If she wanted to go out on a date with Lance, then it was her prerogative. It was the *wrong* decision, but he wasn't going to tell her that.

"Perfect. Write down your address for me. Walker, you got a pen?"

Walker handed Tara a pen, and she jotted her address on a napkin. She handed it to Lance. "Here you go."

"Okay, I'll see you tomorrow at six." Lance

hurried away—without ever saying a word of apology to Tara.

"What are you doing, sis? Why give him another chance?" Walker scrubbed the wooden bar top vigorously, though he'd just wiped it a few minutes ago.

"You heard him. He got tied up. It happens. It happens to us here at work, too."

"But I've never left anyone waiting without so much as a simple phone call." Walker's eyes flashed.

"Can we just drop it? I'm a grown woman and I can make my own decisions."

"Yes, you can. Let's eat." Joey shook his head, just barely, at Walker, who bobbed his head slightly in silent agreement to let it drop. The server showed up just in time to break the tension. Kind of.

They ate their meals, and he didn't tell her he'd already eaten at five. She didn't need to know that or eat her meal alone. She sat quietly through the meal and refused his offer to walk her home.

She slid off her stool and headed out as he sat and finished his beer.

"Never could understand her fascination

with that guy." Walker watched his sister leave. "Wish she would have said a flat-out no to going out with him tomorrow."

"She gets to make her own decisions."

"She does. But she made the wrong decision about Lance. But then, she never does listen to me." Walker scowled and went over to another customer.

Lance just better show up tomorrow and treat Tara like she deserved to be treated. The guy probably didn't even know how to treat a woman as special as Tara. Or any woman. The girls in high school all fawned over him and thought he was so great. And Lance loved being in the spotlight with all his adoring fans.

Lance had cheated on his longtime cheerleader girlfriend, Brandy, but Joey never told Tara that. He couldn't destroy her high school crush. But maybe he should have told her back then. Maybe she'd be going into this whole dating Lance thing with open eyes.

Anger swirled through him afresh. But if going out with Lance is what Tara wanted, needed, then he was one hundred percent behind her. Maybe eighty percent. Okay, not at all. But he wanted to support her decision. Wanted her to finally get her date with the guy.

And maybe, if she had that date, she'd see Lance for the jerk he really was, not some glamorized hero of her youth.

CHAPTER 12

Tara still wasn't certain about her decision to go out with Lance tonight, not that she'd let Walker know it. But there was the powerful pull from her past. How she'd always wanted him to notice her, to ask her out. And now he had. How could she pass up that opportunity?

But then, he stood her up last night. Shouldn't her pride prevent her from saying yes about going out tonight? She pushed the thoughts aside and went back to work.

She looked up from the inventory list as Aspen stepped into the office. "Hey, Aspen."

"Hi. Walker wanted me to check and see if

you needed anything. Things are slowing down a bit from the morning rush."

"No, I'm fine." She looked at Aspen for a moment and laughed. "Walker asked you to come in here and talk to me about Lance, didn't he? Talk me out of going out with him."

"What? No." Aspen blushed. "Okay, he did. But we'll talk only if you want to talk to me."

"There's not much to say. I had a silly schoolgirl crush on him when we were in high school. And now I'm going on a date with him tonight."

"After he was a no-show last night?" Aspen lounged against the doorframe.

"I know, I know. But I just want to know, to *feel* what it's like to go on a date with him. I know it's foolish. I mean, he's this handsome, popular guy. Always dated the head cheerleader, Brandy. Probably still dates the same type of woman. Not someone like me who works in her father's restaurant."

Aspen walked over and dropped into the chair across from her. "Tara, you're selling yourself short. Look at all you do here, all you know. Look how successful the restaurant is."

"That's because of Dad."

"Some of it is because of you and Walker. Changing some things up, but not so much that it's not familiar. Modernizing. Hiring good workers."

They'd tried to modernize a few things, but her dad was a hard no on changing almost anything.

Aspen leaned forward. "Haven't you noticed that your dad is actually taking some time off? That's because of all you do here now. And Walker said that craft beer you found is our number one selling beer now."

She frowned. "Dad did take a day off on Tuesday, didn't he?"

"He did. And really, Tara, you are so beautiful. Who wouldn't want to go out with you? I'm surprised you don't have a long line of men waiting to date you."

She laughed. "I'm not beautiful. My hair is always a wreck. I hardly know how to do makeup more than throw on some lipstick."

"I envy you your hair. It's wonderful and thick. And you're naturally pretty. You don't need a bunch of makeup."

"I don't think you see the same person as I see in the mirror."

"You're not looking closely enough. Besides, it isn't looks that make a person. It's the whole person. How they treat people. How they act. The full package. I know you've always wanted a date with him. Walker explained all that. But Lance... he might not be the man you think he is."

"Maybe, but there's something inside me that wants to have the experience I've always dreamed of. To go out with him."

"Then you go. And you have fun. He's lucky you said yes, and he's lucky to have someone as great as you go out with him."

"You're being too nice." Tara wasn't sure she believed all that Aspen was saying about her.

"No, I'm just being honest." Aspen stood. "And if Lance doesn't realize that and treat you like you deserve tonight, then leave him in the dust. Trust me. I know his type. I've tried to give them all the excuses they needed for not treating me better. Unlike Walker, who treats me like... like I'm really something. Like he cares about me and what I say. Like he's interested in everything about me. You deserve someone like that."

Aspen walked out of the office, and Tara sat staring at the empty doorway. She did deserve someone like that, didn't she? But who's to say that Lance wouldn't be like that? That maybe last night was a fluke, and he did get tied up and felt horrible about it. Although it nagged at her that he hadn't really apologized.

She chewed her bottom lip. And when he'd asked her out, she'd thought he meant just the two of them. Getting to know each other now that they were adults. Not a party at the country club. She was never going to fit in there. Maybe they'd get a chance to slip away and talk. She'd ask him if they could. That's what she would do.

With that resolved, she went back to work on the inventory, then paid some bills, feeling guilty that she was going to miss yet another night's work this evening. But Walker and her mother insisted it was fine. That she should go. Though her brother was less enthusiastic than her mother, but no one had told her mother that Lance stood her up last night.

She sighed and grabbed another bill. Life shouldn't be this complicated, should it?

Aspen went up to the bar and slid on a barstool across from where Walker was working. "So, I talked to Tara."

"And is she still going to go out with Lance? Even after he stood her up?"

"Walker, she's a grown woman and can make her own decisions."

"Yeah, I know that. And I know she's always had a thing for him. But seriously? I was never impressed with the guy, and then when he stood her up, I'm even less impressed."

"It might just be something she needs to do. Get it out of her system. Or see what he's like now."

"I guess."

"You should be supportive of her decisions."

"Even when she's making the wrong one?" He rolled his eyes.

"Even when you disagree. Be supportive."

He let out a long sigh. "You're probably right. Probably. I just hope he doesn't stand her up again."

"I hope that, too." Her phone dinged, and she took it out of her pocket and read the message, excitement swelling through her. "Oh, my sister, Willow, texted and said she and Derek are bringing Eli here soon. She sends me cute photos of him all the time. Look, she sent this one."

She held out her phone so Walker could see the photo.

"Cute nephew."

Her nephew. That still sounded strange to her. "It's still hard for me to believe that she's my sister. Who knew when I got that letter from Magnolia that I'd end up with a sister?"

Her mother, Magnolia, had left quite a surprising letter when she died. Aspen found out she had a sister, a person Magnolia had convinced her was only an imaginary friend, not the real sister her mother had given up for adoption.

"Any luck on finding your dad?"

Ah, the second surprise. Her father hadn't left them. Her mother had packed them up and disappeared in the night, leaving their father behind.

"No, nothing yet. Though Willow said that Derek has a detective working on it. I'm not sure we'll ever find him, though. We don't have much to go on. I'm still so angry that Magnolia said that our father left us when that

115

wasn't the truth. She took us and ran out on him."

"I wish I could do something to help."

She leaned across the counter, grabbed his shoulder, and pulled him close, kissing him quickly. "You do help. Just being supportive."

She looked around to make sure no one had seen her. Walker laughed. "You're allowed to kiss me in public, you know."

"I know." She blushed. But she still wasn't very comfortable with public displays of affection. Or public kisses. Though she would kiss the man all day long if she could.

"I think you should kiss me again. Just so you get used to it," he teased.

She pulled him close and kissed him again. A good long kiss. He finally pulled away, a bemused look on his face. "Ah yeah, you can do that any time you want." He winked, then turned to get back to work.

A smile crept across her cheeks, and she slipped off the stool to get back to work herself. With one last look at Walker and a flutter of her heart, she disappeared into the kitchen.

CHAPTER 13

Tara chose the only dress in her closet remotely appropriate for dinner at the country club, a place she'd never been to but heard a lot about. It was a simple black sleeveless dress, and she hoped it looked classic and timeless, not old and tired. She found a pair of sparkly flats in the back of her closet, with no clue when she bought them or wore them. Though in her final perusal in the mirror, she thought she looked pretty good in the outfit.

But standing here in the entry to the country club, she was uncertain. Maybe everything she'd worn was wrong. Too simple. Too plain.

Lance had on a navy sports coat, fresh white shirt, a tie, and slacks with that precise crease in them that she never could figure out how people could keep looking so crisp. He also looked impossibly handsome.

She smoothed the fabric resting over her hip and clutched her purse tightly.

"Come on, let's go say hello to Mom and Dad." He led her over to his parents. "Mom, Dad, this is Tara. You remember her from high school."

His mother frowned with a dainty shrug of her shoulders. "No, I'm afraid I don't."

"Nice to meet you, Tara." His father smiled, then looked over her shoulder and waved to someone.

"Thanks for having me."

"We had to change the seating arrangements." Mrs. Richards was full of disapproval as she turned to Lance. "You really should have given me more notice."

"And yet, you got it all sorted out. You always do. You're a master at throwing parties." He sent his boyish smile rolling over his mother, and she melted.

"Oh, you. I never could say no to you. Why don't you go over and say hi to Bud Nelson?

He's thinking of moving his company's business to your father's bank."

"Sure thing." Lance turned to her. "You don't mind, do you? I'll be back soon. You can keep yourself busy?"

"Of course."

"And I must go speak to Mrs. Anderson." With that, his mother disappeared along with Lance.

She stood there all alone, looking around the room. She didn't recognize anyone. Not one single person. Not surprising since the country club crowd wasn't exactly the circle of friends she ran with.

She snagged a glass of champagne from a passing server and stood near some potted palms, watching the movers and shakers of Moonbeam do their dance. After twenty minutes, Lance still hadn't returned. She contemplated crossing the room and asking him if they could step outside for a bit, but she wasn't sure she should interrupt him. He was trying to woo that Bud guy over to his father's bank.

Then it was forty minutes, and he hadn't so much as glanced her direction. She set her glass down and snagged another one from a server. At least they were serving great champagne.

Great. That word. And it made her miss Joey. If he were here with her, he'd be making all sorts of comments about the people in this room. And he wouldn't have left her standing all alone, either.

Lance finally came over to her. "Oh, good. You got a glass of champagne. Dad had it flown in specially for this event."

"It's really good." She took another sip as if to prove it. "You think we could take a walk outside?"

"What? No. Let's stay in. Besides, Dad wants me to talk to some more people. I think he might be trying to convince me to move back and work in his bank. I don't know though. I really love the bank I work for in Chicago. And Moonbeam is just so small without much to offer. I guess I could live in Sarasota. Although, compared to Chicago, what does this area of Florida have to offer?"

She stared at him. This area of Florida was wonderful. Full of nice people. Lots to do.

Just then, Brandy LeBow, the former head cheerleader, came up to them. "There you are,

Lance. Daddy said you were here." Brandy stood on tiptoe and kissed Lance's cheek, then slowly turned to look at her and frowned. "I should remember you, shouldn't I? I'm sorry. You are?"

"Tara. Tara Bodine."

Brandy shook her head, and her perfectly curled locks of shoulder-length blonde hair bobbed around her shoulder. "Hm?"

"You know. Her dad owns Jimmy's on the Wharf."

"Oh, right." Brandy gave her what could only be described as a fake smile.

She pasted a big smile on her face in return. "Right. I'm that Tara."

"Oh, Lance. I had such a good time at the charity event your mother threw last night. I swear, she can make any boring old charity seem fun."

Oh, so Brandy was at the event. Maybe it had been less work and more play than she thought.

"She does a good job with it, doesn't she?" Lance glanced across the room. "Oh, there's Dad waving for me. I'll be back." He turned and hurried across the floor.

Brandy stood there for a moment, obviously appraising her. Taking in her simple black dress and sparkly flats... that had lost a couple of sparkles somewhere along the way tonight. "So, you're in town for the reunion?" Brandy's lips curved into another imitation smile.

"No, I live here."

"Really, still? What's there to do here? I couldn't wait to leave."

"I work at Jimmy's."

"Oh, you're a waitress?" Brandy wrinkled her nose.

She didn't bother to correct her. "You know what, Brandy? Could you tell Lance I had to leave?"

"Why sure." This time, Brandy's smile was genuine. "I'd be *glad* to."

Tara swirled around, headed to the nearest exit, and fled outside. She was such a fool. Such. Why had she said yes to Lance? Why had she come tonight? She should have never said yes after he stood her up last night. And tonight wasn't much better. She'd only seen him for mere moments. She paced back and forth on the walkway. She'd have a long walk home in these sparkly shoes that pinched her feet, or she could call someone to pick her up. If she called Walker—or Joey—she'd never hear the end of it.

The door opened behind her, and Lance came out. "There you are. Getting some fresh air? Good idea. Let's take a little walk."

And all thoughts about fleeing were gone when Lance tucked her hand in the crook of his elbow and they headed out along the gently lit path. They stopped after a while and sat on a white bench nestled under a magnolia tree.

"You having a good time?" He stretched out his legs, his pants still precisely creased, with no sign of flattening at his knees.

"Uh, sure." Well, she was now.

"I thought you would. Everyone loves coming to the club. Mom was one of the women heading up the campaign to raise money to redo the club a few years ago. It was getting rather run down in Dad's estimation. He didn't enjoy bringing business associates here anymore. But after a few million dollars in renovations, it looks really nice now, doesn't it?"

"It's very... nicely done." She wouldn't call it nice, though. It was overly done to her taste. When Delbert Hamilton redid The Cabot

Hotel, he stayed true to its original style but updated it slightly and put in more light. She loved what he did. But this country club just screamed *look at me*. Totally overdone in her opinion, but she didn't think that's what Lance wanted to hear.

"You look lovely tonight. Have I told you that?" He smiled at her.

Her heart melted as a smile swept across her mouth. "Thank you."

"We should go back inside. Dinner will be starting. We don't want to upset Mother by being late."

She didn't want to go inside. She wanted to sit out here forever with just Lance. Far away from the crowds. But she rose and followed him back inside. She sat by his side at dinner, noticing Brandy across the large round table, glaring at her. Too bad, so sad, Brandy. Lance is with *me* tonight.

She swept her glance around the people seated at their table. Some of the dresses the women wore probably cost more than a couple months' rent at her apartment. She looked down at her simple black dress that just earlier tonight she had kind of liked how she looked in it. The people around her talked about business deals and trips to Europe and the Caribbean. The women gushed over a new designer shop that opened in Sarasota. She felt helplessly and hopelessly out of place. These were not her friends, her people. They were all about show and who knew who and trying to outdo each other with their stories.

The dinner finally, thankfully, ended and she and Lance walked out to his car. "Aren't you glad you came? It was a fantastic evening, wasn't it?" He gave her his impossible-to-resist smile.

She just smiled in return as she climbed into her side of the car, noticing he didn't come around and open the door for her. But she was capable. She didn't need help. She tugged the door closed. He drove her back to her apartment and walked her to her door.

She stood at the door, wondering if she should ask him in. What would he think of her apartment that she'd spent a good hour cleaning this afternoon and trying to make it look nicer than it was? Fresh flowers in a vase. She'd even hung two pictures. But she was sure he lived in some fancy condo in Chicago and would think her apartment was small and drab.

"I have to run. I'm meeting my father and a few men at the club in Sarasota for cigars and bourbon."

"Okay." That answered that question. No chance to ask him in.

Then he leaned close to her. She held her breath. He brushed a light kiss on her lips. "See ya." He flashed another irresistible smile, then turned away and hurried off to his car.

Lance Richards kissed her.

Lance. Richards. Kissed. Her.

She reached her hand up to her lips, feeling a bit foolish as a wide grin spread across her face. Okay, it had barely been a kiss. Just the lightest brush of his lips, but a kiss nonetheless. She wished she could jump back in time and tell her sixteen-year-old self that she just needed to be patient. That Lance Richards *would* eventually kiss her.

CHAPTER 14

The next morning, Joey sat out on his porch, sipping coffee, wondering how Tara's big date had gone. As if he hadn't spent all last night doing the exact same thing. He'd tried to do some work but eventually closed his laptop, unable to concentrate. Then he spent he didn't know how long just pacing the floor, stewing. Though maybe he should have gone to Jimmy's to sit and wait in case she got stood up again. But that probably hadn't happened. Surely Lance wouldn't stand her up twice, would he?

Maybe she'd figured out what a jerk he was. Or was she still hopelessly under his spell? What did Lance have that caused all the women to be so infatuated with him? He frowned.

"Good morning, Joey." Rose walked up to his bottom step.

"Morning."

"You looked deep in thought."

"I was just pondering what caused people to like certain people. Fall for them. People who are totally wrong for them." He shook his head. "Deep thoughts for an early morning."

Rose climbed the steps and leaned against the railing. "There's no accounting for who we fall in love with. My Emmett? My father absolutely forbade me to see him. Emmett had a reputation of being a bad boy, or so my dad thought. But I saw the other side of him. The kindhearted side. I believe I fell in love with him the first time I saw him."

"But it sounds like Emmett was really a good guy. What if the guy isn't? What if he's shallow, and self-centered, and… just a not good person?"

"Then whoever you're worried about will have to figure that out for themselves. You won't change their mind if they think they're in love."

"I just don't want her to get hurt."

Rose smiled. "It's one of those life lessons that we have to learn for ourselves. Sometimes we get hurt when we fall for someone. And sometimes, if we're very, very lucky, we fall for the right person at the right time and live happily ever after. Like my Emmett and me."

"He's gone now?" he asked quietly, seeing the pain in the corners of her eyes.

"He is. And I miss him terribly. But I wouldn't trade a single moment I spent with him to avoid this pain I have now."

"I'm sorry for your loss."

"It is a great loss, but I still feel him with me. And I'm ever grateful for our life together." She pushed off the railing. "I hope your friend figures out what it is she wants. What's right for her."

"Thanks, Rose. I do, too."

Rose headed off to the office, and he sat pondering all she'd said. Rose was right. He did have to let Tara work her way through her feelings for Lance. Even if he could see clearly that Lance was wrong for her. Lance would never appreciate her the way he did. Never figure out how special she was.

He stood and drained the last of his coffee.

He needed to do something to tamp down this nervous energy he had. No time like the present to go to Beachside Bookshop. He wondered if it had changed much. Maybe if he picked up a good book, he'd keep his mind off Tara and Lance.

He headed down the sidewalk, slowly wandering down street to street until he hit Magnolia. He reached the bookstore and pushed inside, pleased to see that it still looked much the same. A bit larger. They must have expanded. And a coffee bar was tucked over at the side with comfortable chairs scattered around. The familiarity of the shop surrounded him like a hug from a friend.

"Good morning," a woman greeted him.

"Good morning." He headed over to the desk. "Is Mrs. Wetherby here?" He'd love to see her again.

"No, she retired. I took over the store from her."

He looked at her closely, then smiled. "Collette?"

"Yes." She stared at him for a moment, then a grin of recognition spread over her face. "Joey

Duffy. I remember you. Thrillers and adventure books."

"That's me." He smiled.

"You must be in town for the reunion."

"I am. And a friend recommended I try a book by Rob Bentley."

"Ah, our local author. He's a wonderful writer. Here, let me show you his books. I have a table displaying them. We get a lot of requests." She led him to a small table stacked with books. "Choose what you like. I better go help that other customer. She looks a bit lost."

He read the descriptions on Rob's books and picked out two of them in hardcover. That should keep him occupied. Collette checked him out. "Come back again if you have time. On Saturdays, we have sweet tea and cookies in the courtyard."

"I'll try. Good seeing you again." He pushed out the door and hurried back to the cottages, eager to start one of Rob's books. Eager to keep his mind occupied and his thoughts in check.

Collette stood in the back of the bookstore, shelving a new order of books that had just been delivered. She straightened the shelves as she moved along and refiled some books that were in the wrong place. That happened when customers would grab a book to look at, but then not buy it. Sometimes they got put back in the wrong place. It was a constant battle to keep the books organized. She put a romance book back on the shelf in alphabetical order by author—because she was certain that D came before F.

"Hey, you."

She couldn't help her wide smile as she twirled around to see Mark standing there with a bouquet of flowers in his hands. "Mark, what are you doing here?"

"Taking a long weekend." He grinned at her. "Thought I'd spend it with you."

She threw her arms around him. "I'm so happy to see you." She kissed him quickly, then glanced around to see if anyone was watching them. "But I have to work this weekend."

"I might have called Jody and asked if she'd cover for you. Besides, you also have that new worker you just hired. You said she was catching on quickly, right? Jody said they'd be fine. She was tickled you'd be taking some time off."

"Really?"

"Really. You've just got the day shift tomorrow, then she has the weekend and you're all mine. I hope you don't mind that I called her. I wanted to surprise you."

"I'm not going to complain about that." She took the flowers he handed her and buried her nose in them, reveling in their sweet yet spicy scent.

"Good, because I have plans. Going to happy hour at Blue Heron Cottages tomorrow. A beach day on Saturday, or we could go to some of those antique shops you like to browse through. Really, as long as I'm with you, I don't care what we do. I got a room at Blue Heron Cottages, but I want to spend every waking moment with you."

"It all sounds wonderful. I miss you when you're back at home." She smiled up at him, memorizing his face as if she hadn't just seen him six days ago. "How's work going?"

"Really well." His eyes lit up. "I've had some new ideas for displays that are paying off. Mr. Mason hired two new workers, so that's why it was easier to get time off. He said that since I've hardly taken any time off in all the years I've worked at the hardware store, I should make up for lost time." He brushed her cheek with a kiss. "So I took him up on his offer."

Jody walked up to them. "Ahem, sorry to interrupt. I see you surprised her." Jody grinned. "But why don't you two lovebirds go ahead and leave? Spend some time together. I've got things here and I'll lock up at closing time."

"You sure?"

Jody laughed. "I'm positive. All you've done the last week is talk about Mark. Say how much you missed him."

"She did?" Now it was Mark's turn to grin.

"I might have mentioned you once or twice." She tried to hide her smile. "Okay, if you're sure you have everything covered."

"I'm sure."

She took Mark's hand and led him upstairs to her apartment, where they could have some time alone. As soon as she closed the apartment door behind her, Mark pulled her into his arms. "I've been waiting all week to do this." He kissed her gently, then deepened the kiss.

Her heart fluttered, and she steadied herself

by holding onto his arms. When he finally pulled away, she said, "I can see you haven't forgotten how to kiss."

He threw back his head and laughed. "I plan on getting a lot of practice this weekend."

"I'm just the woman for you to practice on."

CHAPTER 15

Tara went over to her parents' house late Thursday afternoon to help her mom get ready for the barbecue. She found her mother in the kitchen, deep into preparations for dinner. "I got the bag of ice you wanted."

"Thanks. Can you put it in the cooler?"

As soon as she stepped outside, a smile of amusement tugged at the corners of her mouth. Never one to miss an opportunity to decorate, her mother had scattered lanterns around the backyard and strung twinkle lights between the trees. A large table was set with a bright floral tablecloth. The grill stood ready at the side for her father to do his magic on the steaks her mother had picked out.

She dumped the ice over the beer cans and soda and headed back inside. "What else can I do?"

"Could you chop up those tomatoes for the salad?"

She headed over to the large cutting board and grabbed a knife. "Backyard looks great."

"Thank you. I wanted it to look festive for Joey. My heart breaks for him for the loss of his parents. I just wanted to do something to cheer him up."

"I'm sure he appreciates it. He always loved coming over here for dinner. His parents worked late so often and he mostly ate alone at his house."

"His parents were lovely people, but they were the type who thought work came before everything else." Her mother's face held a gentle, disapproving look.

She and Walker had been lucky. Even with running the restaurant, their parents had always made it plain that family came first. She glanced over at her mother, who concentrated on seasoning the steaks with her magic combination of spices. "Hey, Mom, thanks for doing this. It means a lot to me."

She looked up in surprise. "Of course. Joey is family. Family does what they can when one of us is having a hard time."

Her mother really was the nicest person on the planet. Always thinking of others. A pang flicked through her, just thinking of losing her mother like Joey had lost his. She couldn't bear it. She went over and hugged her. "Love you, Mom."

Her mother hugged her back. "What's this for?"

"Just wanted you to know I love you and you're the best mom ever."

Her mother smiled. "I love you too, honey."

She chased away the thoughts of losing her mother and went back to her task, sliding the knife through a juicy, plump tomato.

Her mother went over to the oven and pulled out two pies. Apple pie, Joey's favorite. She settled the pies on a cooling rack. "With Joey and Walker's appetite, I figured one was not enough. Besides, this way I can send some home with Joey."

See, her mom was the nicest person ever.

Her mother put the oven mitts down and

turned to her. "So, how was your date with Lance last night?"

She blushed slightly, remembering the kiss. "Oh, it was nice."

"Did you enjoy the country club?"

A gentle laugh escaped her. "No, not really. I didn't know anyone, and they were… stuffy. I didn't really fit in. And Brandy was there—do you remember her from high school days?—she shot dagger looks at me all night for being there with Lance."

Her mother shook her head. "That crowd is sometimes pretty full of themselves. But you should never feel like they're better than you. They aren't."

She paused, holding the knife above another tomato. "I don't think I felt like that. I just felt out of place. Like my clothes were wrong, and I had nothing to contribute to all their conversation about world travel."

"You still had a good time?"

She nodded. But she wasn't going to tell her mother about the kiss. Or Walker, for that matter. The teasing would be endless with her brother.

Voices sounded from the front of the house.

Walker and Aspen, her father, and Joey came walking into the kitchen.

"Found Joey outside," Walker said as he came over and swiped a piece of tomato.

"Walker, wash your hands," their mother commanded. "Then how about you go out and help your father with the grill?"

"What can I do to help?" Joey asked.

"Take Tara outside and you two grab drinks. I'm almost finished up here. You go enjoy yourselves."

She headed outside with Joey and they dug deep in the ice for cold beers. "Let's go out on the dock." She led the way out to the long dock and they settled on the heavy wooden Adirondack chairs. She took a sip of her beer and turned to him. "This is nice, isn't it? Just like old times. Except with beer." She clinked her can against his and grinned.

"It is. So nice." Joey leaned back in the familiar chair, stretching out his legs. "Oh, wow. I've missed this so much. How many hours do you think we spent sitting out here?"

He smiled at the memories flitting through his mind.

"A bazillion." Her lips tipped into a smile, her eyes twinkling. "Or more."

"Right, it was out here on these chairs, or sitting on the porch swing at my house."

"Love that porch swing."

Not sure he wanted to know the answer, he took a sip of his beer and asked nonchalantly, "So, how was your date last night?"

"It was nice."

Was nice a good thing or a bad thing? Was it really nice or only kinda nice? "So you had fun?"

"Uh, sure. I mean, I didn't know anyone but Lance."

"And his parents."

"They... they didn't remember me."

Of course not. Their son had only gone to school with her his entire childhood. Now what to say to her? He took another sip of his beer. "So, are you going out with him again?"

"We don't have any plans."

That statement made him ridiculously happy. Though he had hoped she would see

Lance for what he really was. But that didn't appear to have happened.

"You're not going with him to the bonfire?"

She shook her head. "No, I want to go with you. Just like old times. We've gone to so many bonfires together."

"We have." A grin spread across his face, and delight spread through him. She wanted to go with *him*, not Lance. "It will be great to go to one with you again." Score one for Joey, none for Lance.

"It will be fun. I'm looking forward to it. Haven't been to a bonfire on the beach in ages."

"I'll come over to your place and we'll walk to it?"

"Of course. Is there any other way?" She flashed him a smile.

He looked out over the bay, content. This was right where he wanted to be. Here, sitting on the dock with Tara. They sat and talked until Mrs. Bodine rang the dinner bell and he laughed out loud. "I've missed that old bell."

"Some things don't change at the Bodines'. Like the dinner bell for a big family dinner."

He jumped up and held out a hand for her.

She took it and he pulled her to her feet. She kept her hand comfortably in his as they walked back up to the house. He reluctantly let her go when they got to the table and slipped into their seats.

Mr. Bodine served up the steaks, and they passed around the bowls of all the food Mrs. Bodine had made. A large salad. Green beans. A pasta dish. Freshly baked bread. This was better than the finest five-star restaurant with the highest-rated meals. As far as he was concerned, this was heaven.

They ate their meal while the sunset threw a showy display of colors and the lanterns and twinkle lights cast an enchanting glow around the area. Or maybe he was just on a rush of happiness and contentment. The evening seemed magical to him.

After clearing up the dishes, they all sat around the fire pit and roasted marshmallows for s'mores. He sat back and listened to Walker tease Tara, his arm draped around Aspen's shoulder. Mr. Bodine held his wife's hand, smiling intimately at her and squeezing her hand. Joey sat beside Tara on a glider, slowly moving back and forth in a smooth, regular rhythm. She leaned against his shoulder. He smiled at her, and she rewarded him with a smile full of affection and contentment. He swept his gaze around the circle of people gathered in the firelight. This was about as perfect as it could get.

A tiny pang jabbed at his heart. He never had this with his family, and never would. The Bodines were a family in a league of their own. Genuine. Giving. Loving. And yet, they never made him feel like an outsider. They included him as one of their own.

Tara reached over and touched his hand. "You having a good time?"

His emotions almost choked him, but he managed to get out the words. "Best day ever."

"Great." A captivating smile settled on her lips.

And suddenly, he wanted to lean close and kiss her. His pulse quickened, his breath caught, and he stared at her lips.

What?

Where had that come from? She was his *friend*. And yet…

Tara accepted Joey's offer to walk her home after the barbecue. He said his thank-yous to her parents, and they headed out. She held lightly to his arm as they strolled in and out of the lamplight lining the sidewalks.

"I had such a wonderful time with your family tonight."

"Mom loved having you." She looked at his face, peaceful and content. The worry lines that were etched on his face when he arrived in Moonbeam were smoothed away. Good. Her plan to make him forget his problems and lessen his pain seemed to be working.

"It kind of felt like old times, didn't it?" He placed his hand over hers resting on his arm. "We had such a great childhood growing up here, didn't we?"

"There's that great again." She grinned. "But yes, we did. I miss those days sometimes. Carefree. Sneaking off to the beach for a day of doing nothing at all."

He paused under a lamppost. "Adulting is hard sometimes, isn't it?"

She reached up and touched his cheek. "I know this has been a difficult year for you. I'm sorry. I hope coming back here helped. Seeing people who care about you."

A flicker of pain crossed his eyes, but he quickly hid it. "It has been good coming back here. Seeing you. Seeing your family. Your parents always treated me like I was family."

"You are family to us," she assured him. "Come on." She tugged his hand. "We should get going. I have an early day tomorrow. Working at Jimmy's before we head out to the bonfire tomorrow evening. You ready for all the excitement?"

"I don't know. I'm pretty certain nothing they have planned for the weekend will beat this night with your family."

She loved seeing him happy. Seeing him relaxed. It had been a successful evening. And she'd enjoyed herself, too. She kept her hand in his as they headed back to her apartment and he walked her to her door. "Thank you, Tara. I really did have a wonderful time."

"I'm glad you could come. I had a good time, too. I wish…"

"You wish what?" He cocked his head to one side, his eyes questioning her.

"I wish you didn't have to leave so soon. I

could get used to you being here. Having you around. I've missed you."

"Missed you, too. I didn't realize how much until I returned." He stood there, his gaze burning into her, his eyes locked with hers for what felt like an eternity. Then suddenly he took a step back and cleared his throat. "Ah, I should go."

She nodded, any words she might have said stuck in her throat. He spun around and hurried off, disappearing around a corner. She stepped inside and flicked on the lamp. A soft glow illuminated the room.

The empty room that didn't feel like home to her. She really should fix that.

She crossed to the kitchen and put on the kettle to make a cup of chamomile tea because oddly, her nerves were a bit jangled. But they shouldn't be after the nice, relaxed evening.

And yet... something about the way Joey had looked at her before he left unnerved her. The craziest thought flashed through her mind. Had he been thinking about *kissing* her?

No, they were just friends. That was all.

She shook her head, clearing away the absurd thoughts, and reached for a box of assorted herbal teas. She riffled through and pulled out a chamomile, tearing open the packet and placing it in her favorite floral teacup. She poured the hot water and carried the tea over to the sofa, plopped down, and kicked off her shoes.

She and Joey were *friends*. Just friends.

But why had he looked at her so intently? And why had her heart skipped a beat when he did?

CHAPTER 16

R ose sat on the beach in her favorite spot, watching the sky lighten and enjoying the soft breeze. In the distance, a lone man walked along the water's edge, bending down occasionally then tossing something into the water. Ah, a shell tosser. Just like her Emmett. As he got closer, she realized it was Joey and lifted a hand in a wave.

As he walked up, she patted the sand beside her, and he dropped down next to her. "Morning, Rose."

"Good morning, Joey. Out for an early walk, I see."

"I'm getting into quite a routine here. I'd forgotten how much I enjoy an early morning beach walk. Even when I was a kid and all the other kids wanted nothing more than to sleep in on the weekends, I'd get up early and spend time at the beach." He looked out to sea, then back at her. "I'll miss this when I leave. The walks. The sunrises." He paused and his mouth tipped up in a comfortable, friendly smile. "Miss chatting with you."

"It is hard to leave this, I know. That's why I haven't headed home yet. I keep extending my stay. Maybe you could extend yours a bit, too."

"Maybe. But I have things I need to do back home."

A rueful laugh escaped her. "Yes, don't we all? But so far, that hasn't made me return home."

"I'm sure you'll know when it's the right time to leave."

"You're probably right." She picked up a shell and placed it in her hand, tracing over its lines. "So, how was your night last night? What did you do?"

"The Bodines had me over for dinner. I had the best time. They've always made me feel like one of the family. I... I like that." He looked over at her. "Do you have kids? Other family?"

"Ah, no kids. Emmett and I were never blessed with any. It's just me now." But that wasn't quite the truth, was it?

"We're quite a pair, aren't we? All alone with no family."

She let out a sigh, unwilling to lie, even lie by omission. "I'm not quite alone. I do have a sister. But we don't see each other. Haven't for years."

He looked at her intently and frowned. "And would you like that to change?"

She shook her head. "I honestly don't know. Some things just can't be forgotten. Not even years later."

"Maybe, but it might be worth a try."

She smiled at him. "Very practical advice."

"You could take it." He shrugged. "Or not. I'm not one to really know much about family dynamics. I just know that I'd give anything to have a family like the Bodines."

"I bet you'll have that one day. Some day when you meet the right woman."

"Maybe." He pushed off the sand. "I better head in. I've got a busy day. Need to get some work done before the reunion bonfire tonight."

"You should come to happy hour this

evening before you go to the bonfire. Violet has it every Friday in the courtyard."

"I should probably be able to make it."

"Great, I'll see you there."

He walked toward the cottages and she stayed put, scooping up handfuls of sand, and letting it sift through her fingers, burying the shell she'd picked up.

Her sister.

Pauline. She wasn't even sure where her sister lived now. It wasn't like they sent Christmas cards or anything. She'd tried once, after Emmett died, to find Pauline by searching on the internet, but didn't have much luck. And she hadn't been sure if that was a good thing or not.

Pauline. Her younger sister. She squeezed her eyes shut against the memories. They'd been inseparable growing up. Only eleven months apart in age. They did everything together. Shared their clothes, their friends, only a year apart in school. Pauline had stood up with her when she married Emmett. Then all that had changed. Gone up in a storm of disappointment and anger. Forty years. She hadn't seen Pauline in forty years. Not even when their father died.

She thought for sure her sister would show up for the funeral, but no. No sign of her.

To tell the truth, she wasn't even sure if her sister was alive anymore. Except for this feeling deep inside that Pauline was still out there somewhere.

She got up and walked down to the water's edge, letting the waves lap at her feet, then rush back down the gentle slope of the beach to be embraced by the next wave. Maybe Joey was right. Maybe she should try again to find Pauline.

But then, what would that help? Some things couldn't be forgiven. Or forgotten. Or could they?

She looked out at the sea, but it gave her no answer.

Violet slowly swept her gaze around the courtyard. Everything looked ready for her guests. She really enjoyed her Friday happy hours and loved that some of her friends from town would drop by and enjoy the weekly tradition with her. The beer and soda were iced. The white wine was resting in an ice bucket, and a couple of bottles of red wine were open and breathing on the serving table.

In a moment of inspiration—or maybe craziness—she'd watched a video online on how to make a charcuterie board and tried her hand at it. It hadn't turned out as well as the one in the video, but it was *kind of* pretty looking.

She'd made a large pitcher of lemonade for the family staying in the blue cottage with three little girls and put out bowls of pretzels and animal crackers, hoping the girls might enjoy those.

Rob walked up to her and gave her a quick, one-armed hug. "Hey, sis. Can I do anything to help?"

"No, I've got it all. Just grab yourself a beer. Is Evelyn coming?"

"No, she's working at the cafe."

"Hey, Violet."

She looked up to see Collette and Mark walking up."Hey, you two."

Rose crossed the courtyard and joined them with a bouquet of fresh flowers in an old mason jar. "Here, these are for you. I was in town and that new floral shop was setting up. I met the owner, Daisy. She seems very nice if a bit overwhelmed right now. She's not officially open yet. I think maybe sometime next week?"

"Thank you." Violet reached for the flowers and set them on the serving table. "That looks nice, doesn't it? And it will be nice to have a floral shop in town."

"I can't resist using old mason jars for vases." Rose shook her head and turned to Mark and Collette "Mark, I didn't know you were going to be in town this weekend."

"Surprise trip to… well, surprise Collette." He glanced at Collette with a look that said he was obviously smitten with her. Good for him. Good for Collette. Two nice people who deserved each other and the happiness they could find.

"Where'd you find the old mason jars? I love them for vases, too." Collette asked.

"Luckily, I found a few when I was browsing in Bella's Vintage Shop over on Belle Island the other day."

"We were thinking of heading over there tomorrow. I…" Collette laughed and looked at Mark. "I need another bookshelf."

"But of course, you do." Mark shook his head, but his eyes twinkled.

"Another bookshelf is always a good idea. You can never have too many," Rose answered in agreement as she poured herself a glass of wine.

"See, you should listen to Rose. She is wise." Collette nudged Mark and smiled.

The family from the blue cottage came out, and the three girls, all outfitted in matching dresses, came over. The oldest girl twirled around in front of Violet. "See my new dress?"

"It's very pretty."

"And my sisters had to get the same one." She let out a long-suffering sigh with a slight pout on her face. "They always want to be like me."

"Mama, can I have those cookies that look like bears?" the smallest girl asked.

"Yes, if you also take a carrot stick." Their mother poured them lemonade and got them each a plate with a carrot, some pretzels, and a few cookies.

"There's a beanbag toss game over at the edge of the courtyard if you girls would like to play that after your snack."

"Can we, Mama?" The youngest girl twirled around, clapping her hands. She stumbled slightly, and her father scooped her up in his arms.

"Yes, of course."

Pleased that she'd made the right choice for the girls, Violet watched as the family went over and sat at a small grouping of chairs.

She spied Joey standing on the steps of his cottage. "Come on over," she called out.

He loped across the distance. "Quite a spread you have here."

"Grab what you'd like. Beer and soda in the cooler, wine on the table."

He walked over and grabbed a soda, then came back to join them.

Melody and Ethan walked across the courtyard. "Hey, everyone," Melody said.

Violet was pleased to see the two of them together. Now, if Ethan would only get the nerve up to ask Melody out on a date…

These happy hours had turned out just like she'd imagined. Her guests, her friends, all enjoying an hour or so of camaraderie. Rob leaned close to her. "You've done good here, sis. I'm proud of you."

"You mean since when I first said I bought the resort and you rolled your eyes at me and just *knew* I'd made the wrong decision?"

He laughed. "Yes, since then. But I was... dare I say it? Wrong."

"Then that means I was... what is that word... right?"

"Don't let it go to your head. It doesn't happen often." He grinned at her.

She looked around the courtyard again, filled with guests and friends. This is what she'd imagined when she bought the small resort. Only it had turned out even better.

"Hey, Robbie?"

"Hm?" He paused, his beer halfway to his mouth.

"You're not bad for a brother." She grinned at him and walked over to check and see if the cooler needed more ice.

"Love ya, sis," he called after her.

CHAPTER 17

Mark saw Melody move away from Ethan and go talk to Rose. His perfect chance to go chat with him. "Excuse me for a few minutes," he whispered to Collette. She nodded and went back to talking to Violet.

Mark headed over to where Ethan was standing, sipping on a beer. "Hey, there."

"Hey, yourself. I see you're now a frequent visitor to Moonbeam."

"That I am." He glanced back toward Collette, watching her talking and laughing with her friends. "All it took was to get my nerve up and decide that Collette was the right woman for me."

"It does look like it worked out for you."

"And have you asked out Melody yet?"

Ethan sighed. "No, not yet. I'm still not sure she'd say yes."

"I thought my last pep talk convinced you to at least try. The worst that could happen is she says no."

"But then it would be awkward between us." Ethan frowned.

"Only if you let it. If I hadn't gotten out of my own way, I'd never be dating Collette. I swear, I've never felt like this about anyone. She makes me extremely happy. I can't imagine my life now without her in it." She brought such joy to his life. He woke up thinking of her, and she was in his last thoughts before he fell asleep. He still couldn't believe his luck that he'd found her.

Ethan glanced over at Melody and said softly, "I can't imagine my life without Melody."

"Then it's time you asked her out." He said the words with authority, hoping Ethan would finally take them to heart.

"I'll think about it."

"If you wait too long, you might miss your chance. I almost missed my chance with Collette. I was foolish. Don't let that happen to you. She accepts me just as I am. With all my faults."

Ethan frowned. "I'm nothing like her husband, John, was. Nothing. She misses him a lot. Still."

Mark glanced over at Melody. It must have been hard to be widowed so young. But maybe Ethan would be good for her. He certainly cared about her. That was obvious to everyone except for Melody. "Maybe that's a good thing that you're different from what he was like. Maybe that's exactly what she needs."

"Maybe." But Ethan's eyes filled with doubt.

Mark stifled a sigh. He'd tried. He really had. But it seemed like there was just no convincing Ethan that now was the right time to ask Melody out.

Melody turned as Ethan walked up to her. "Could I get you more wine?"

She handed her glass to him. "Just a half glass. Thanks."

He returned with a beer for himself and the wine for her. He pressed the glass into her hand.

KAY CORRELL

"I really enjoy coming to Violet's happy hour, but I feel bad that Evelyn is back at the cafe working." Melody took a sip of the wine.

"I thought you said she'd been working a lot since she got back from her honeymoon. Felt like she needed to catch up on things."

"She has. But I still worry about her after her accident. She says she's all recovered, but goodness, she gave us all a scare."

"That she did. And it looked like it took ten years off Rob's life. He was really worried about her."

"But it motivated him to ask her to marry him. That's something good that came out of it all." She glanced over at Rob, talking to Mark, both looking like they belonged in Moonbeam and had lived here forever. Moonbeam had a way of pulling people in and claiming them.

"Yes, that was a nice thing that happened." Ethan looked toward Rob and Mark, then back at her. "Um, I was wondering if I could ask you something."

"Of course." She looked at him and tried to read his expression. Was it... was it fear? She reached out and touched his arm. "What?"

"I was wondering. I mean, I was thinking.

164

Um…" His face reddened, and he wiped his hand on his hip, then slid it into his pocket. Then took it back out.

"Ethan, just say it." She reached out and took his hand. He stared down at their hands, entranced. "Ethan?"

He finally looked back up at her. "Would…" He cleared his throat. "Would you go out with me? On a date I mean. Like out to dinner or something?" The question came out in a rush like one long word smooshed together.

She looked at him in shock. He'd just asked her out? She licked her lips, trying to find the right words. Uncertain how she wanted to answer him. She hadn't dated anyone since her husband died, and she wasn't sure she was ready now. But then, there was no man nicer than Ethan Chambers. He'd become her friend in the last year or so.

She realized she was just standing there, stunned, not answering. "Um…"

"No, that's okay. It was just an idea. A silly one, probably." His face darkened to a crimson red. "Forget I said anything."

"No, Ethan. It's not a silly idea," she whispered. "I'm just not sure I'm ready to date.

I haven't even considered it. I... I still feel married to John, even though he's gone."

"I understand. I'm sorry. I just thought maybe... Sorry, it was wrong to even ask you." He stared down at his beer.

"Can you give me a little time to think it over? Maybe get used to the idea of dating again?"

"Yes, I could do that. For sure." A bit of relief showed on his face. "You take all the time you need. Then you let me know."

"Yes, I promise. We'll talk about it again soon."

Rob and Violet walked up, and soon Rose joined them and she was surrounded by conversation and laughter. But all she could think about was Ethan's question. Would she go out with him? Her heart pounded in her chest at the thought. She hadn't dated since she was a teen, before marrying John. And it felt a bit disloyal to John to even be thinking about it. She kept glancing at Ethan, but he was avoiding looking at her.

Now she'd probably bungled her friendship with Ethan, too. What a mess. She took another swallow of her wine.

"You okay?" Violet leaned close. "You look a bit lost in thought."

"Oh, sorry. No, I'm fine." She pasted on a bright smile. "Having a lovely time." Just lovely. Although the life she'd carefully mapped out for herself after John's death had just been pushed off kilter.

CHAPTER 18

Tara set down a stack of menus on the hostess stand.

"Are you and Lance going to the bonfire?" Aspen slipped the menus onto the shelf on the backside of the stand.

"No, I'm going with Joey."

"Oh?" Aspen quickly covered up her surprised expression.

She wasn't going to admit that Lance hadn't asked her to go with him. Hadn't even said a word about seeing her at the bonfire. Or seeing her again at all, for that matter. Though maybe he just assumed she'd be there. That was probably it.

She suppressed a sigh. Look at her. Mooning

after Lance, just like when she was a silly high school girl. Would she ever get over him?

But then... why had he kissed her? What did that mean?

She shoved her confused thoughts away. Anyway, she'd have more fun going with Joey, right? She'd feel comfortable and could just be herself. "No, Joey and I thought it would be fun to go together. Just like old times." She glanced at her watch. She should head out soon and get ready.

"Go on. I've got this." Aspen tilted her head toward the doorway. "Go and have a great time."

"Okay, thanks." She turned and headed to the door, hoping to escape any questions from Walker. He hadn't asked her about tonight, and she'd rather keep it that way.

She hurried to her apartment and took a nice cool shower, washing away the stickiness of the day and the faint aroma of fried food. She took her towel and wiped the steam off the mirror and there was her thick, unruly hair mocking her. She grabbed her hairdryer and began the long process of drying it. After trying to tame it with a round brush and the dryer, hoping to make it lie in nice, gentle waves, she gave up. Sighing, she pulled it up and twisted it into a knot, securing it tightly. Of course, a few locks of hair fell out as they always did.

She walked over to her closet, wondering what in the world she had to wear that looked casual, but nice. Lance would probably be in nice shorts and possibly even a button-down shirt with the sleeves rolled up. He was a classy dresser like that. She didn't want to dress up too much, but she didn't feel like shorts and a t-shirt were the right outfit either. Even though every bonfire she'd ever gone to with Joey, she wore exactly that. And why was she worried about what Lance was wearing? She was going with Joey.

Her indecisiveness annoyed her. Annoyed her a lot. When had she become a person not confident in her choices?

Oh, she knew exactly when. The day Lance strode back into town.

She finally decided on a pair of black capris and a floral blouse. Casual, but a bit nicer than shorts and t-shirt. She dug in the closet for some black canvas slip-ons and decided the look was perfect. Maybe.

Joey left happy hour and headed over to Tara's. He'd had a great time at Violet's get-together. Everyone was friendly and welcoming. For the first time in a long time, he was starting to feel at home. But Moonbeam wasn't his home anymore. Where was his home? He frowned. He really had no desire to stay in California. He could sell his condo and move elsewhere.

He should try Philadelphia again, or Boston. He had connections there. Maybe he could find a new job. Maybe that would stop the restlessness he felt these days. Maybe.

Time enough to figure that out later. For now, he just planned on enjoying all the reunion activities and spending time with Tara. He reminded himself that what Tara wanted was to spend time with Lance. He'd see if he could make that happen, even though it pained him.

He got to her door and knocked.

She opened the door, and his eyes widened. "Wow, you look great." The black capris hugged her thin waist and long legs. The floral blouse brought a pop of color. Her hair was pulled back, but adorable ringlets that he was sure annoyed her had escaped, framing her face.

"Uh, thanks." She shoved a lock of hair behind her ear.

"You ready to go?"

"I am." She stepped out, locked the door, and slipped the key into her pocket. "Let's go the long way, past your old house, past my parents'. It will feel more like old times that way."

"Sounds like a plan to me." Though he wasn't certain he wanted to see his old house again. And again. He'd seen it when he first got here and then last night, of course. Now again? But if that was what Tara wanted, that was what they would do.

They strolled along the sidewalks and Tara seemed lost in thought. Probably thinking about Lance. He smothered a sigh of annoyance. Lance was what Tara wanted, he reminded himself.

They reached the street where they'd both lived as kids and slowed down. "The porch swing is still there," she said as they paused in front of his house.

"It is."

173

She turned to him, inclining her head, another wisp of hair falling loose. "We did have the best childhood. But do you ever wish... ever wish you could go back? When things were simpler? Maybe make some different choices?"

He caught himself just before reaching out and brushing back that wisp of her hair that fascinated him. "No, not really. I mean, we don't ever get that chance. Would you make different choices?"

"I... I don't know. Maybe I'd do something different than work at Jimmy's? Maybe. Especially because I feel like Dad never likes anything I suggest to update the place a little. But I felt like I didn't have a choice. It was always decided I would work there." She shook her head. "I would change one thing, though."

"What's that?"

"I never would have let you move away." She bumped her shoulder against his, grinning, and grabbed his hand, tugging him forward. "Come on. There's a bonfire to get to."

They walked down the sidewalks, the same route they'd taken all those years ago. So many times. So many memories danced through his mind. They reached the beach and paused on the edge of it. "Quite a crowd." It rivaled the crowds they'd had back in their youth.

"Yes, look at everyone." She stood beside him, scanning the crowd.

People milled around the growing bonfire. Large coolers were filled with ice, beer, and sodas, lining the edge of the crowd. Just like old times. Well, other than the beer. It was only sodas back then, except for when some of the guys smuggled in beer or liquor. Guys like Lance. He always seemed to scare up a six-pack or two.

He glanced over at Tara as she searched the crowd. Probably looking for Lance. But that was okay. That hadn't really changed since their days as kids. She'd always been watching for Lance.

"Come on, let's join them." He led the way across the sand.

CHAPTER 19

Tara scanned the crowd, looking for Lance. She didn't see him anywhere. Maybe he hadn't even come.

Joey leaned close. "He's over there. On the far side. Standing by Brandy."

Of course, Brandy had found him. Maybe she'd even come here with him. "Who's where?" she asked innocently.

"Nice try." He rolled his eyes. "I'll grab us some beers and we'll wander over that direction."

"Yes, to the beer. No, we don't have to go over there."

"Come on, Tara. You've had a crush on the guy for years. You've had a date with him. Don't let a little thing like Brandy stop you. We're going over there."

Joey disappeared to grab two beers. She stared over at Brandy and Lance. She'd been right. Lance had on nice navy shorts and a pin-striped dress shirt with the sleeves casually rolled up. Brandy had on a red sundress with a navy sweater draped over her shoulders. They looked like they'd coordinated their outfits. She looked down at her simple capris and blouse. Wrong choice.

Joey returned and took her elbow. "Come on, we're going over there." He led her over to the far side of the bonfire. "Oh, hey there, Lance. Didn't see you standing there," Joey said, then turned to wink at her.

"Duffy." Lance's look dismissed Joey. "Tara, hi." But he didn't light up in appreciation of her like Joey had when she opened the door tonight, either. She hadn't missed Joey's look. The look that said he thought she looked great. She could always count on his support.

"Hi, Brandy." She gave the woman what she hoped was a friendly, not pained, smile.

"Tara." The tone of voice was anything but welcoming and warm.

"Getting pretty crowded here," Joey said conversationally.

"Yes, there's a good turnout," Brandy said. "Though I'm not sure why they decided a bonfire was a good idea. I mean, I suggested a nice dinner somewhere. Like the country club. Lance, your parents could have sponsored the event."

"Maybe. But Mom is more into sponsoring charity events and things like that."

"I think the bonfires are fun," she said half because she meant it and half because she wanted to contradict Brandy.

"Oh, maybe when we were kids. But now? They are just so…" Brandy shrugged and flipped her hair back—the same exact move she used to repeat over and over in high school. "They're rather infantile, don't you think?"

"I agree with Tara. I love bonfires." Joey was quick to jump to her defense.

"I'm going to side with Brandy on this one. They might have been fun when we were kids, but now they are a bit boring. We should all go out to eat somewhere. Maybe Portside Grill."

Right, because he'd missed going there when he'd stood her up there this week. She squashed the thought. Joey looked over at her, an eyebrow raised in question. He was silently asking her if she wanted to leave. She knew that. Knew Joey so well that he could ask a question without words.

"I'm staying. I want to say hi to more friends from school." Was she making the wrong decision? Sending Lance off with Brandy?

"I think that's a wonderful idea." Brandy threaded her arm through Lance's, sending Tara a triumphant smile.

"Guess we'll see you kids tomorrow." Lance nodded and turned away.

She heard Brandy talking as they walked away. "That's another thing I thought was a bad idea. The picnic in the park. All the bugs. The flies. And who wants to play horseshoes and volleyball and silly things like that? Haven't we outgrown all that?"

"You okay?" Joey asked.

"Of course. Why wouldn't I be?" But she couldn't keep herself from watching Lance's retreating back and wishing he either would have really asked her directly to go, or he would have stayed here with her.

Joey bumped her lightly with his hip. "Come on. Let's go say hi to everyone."

With one last look at where Lance had disappeared, she followed Joey over to a group of their friends. And she'd been right about one thing. The first question anyone asked her was what she was doing now. "Working at Jimmy's." She pasted on a weak smile each time the question was asked.

Late that night, Joey walked her back to her apartment. "Did you have a good time?" he asked as they approached her door.

"I guess so."

"You could have gone out to eat with Lance, you know."

"I know... but that kind of defeats the purpose of going to our reunion, doesn't it? To leave the bonfire and go somewhere else? Besides, I'm sure he had a lovely time with Brandy." Though the thought irked her.

"Probably." His eyes held a tinge of sympathy. "But you'll see him again tomorrow. At the picnic and at the actual reunion."

She nodded.

"Want me to swing by and pick you up for the picnic tomorrow?"

"Nah, I have to work the morning shift. Can I just meet you there at the park?"

"That'll work." He took a step back. "Had a great time tonight. It was almost like old times, wasn't it?"

"It was." Right down to the fact that Lance barely noticed her.

And the fact that it bothered her annoyed her. When would she ever get over her silly crush on the guy?

CHAPTER 20

Violet hid her surprise when Melody showed up early Saturday morning at the Blue Heron Cottages office. "Hey, you."

"Hi. I was restless and went out for an early walk before work. Ended up this way and thought I'd stop in."

"Rose and I were just going to have some coffee. Care to join us?"

"That sounds nice."

She poured them all coffee and they went out to the porch, settling on the chairs. She loved the now daily morning ritual of coffee with Rose. A nice way to start the day.

"Had a lovely time at the happy hour last night, Violet," Rose said. "It's such a pleasant way to meet the guests and see some of your friends."

"I had a good time, too," Melody said as she set her coffee down on the table beside her. "An interesting time."

"Oh?" Violet cocked her head.

"So… guess what?" Melody asked.

"I give up. Just tell us." Violet looked over as a hint of a blush crept across Melody's face.

"So… while we were here at the happy hour, Ethan asked me out."

"He did? Great." She paused and frowned. "Wait… what did you say?"

"I said… I didn't know."

"You didn't know what?"

"If that was a good idea or not."

"Why wouldn't it be?" Rose leaned forward. "He seems like such a nice young man."

"He is a nice guy. I just don't think…" Melody's voice caught. "I don't think I'm over losing John yet."

"Ah, that." Rose's eyes creased with a smidgen of pain framing them. "I'm not sure we ever get over that. I'm sure I'll never get over losing my Emmett. But we can't let losing our husbands cause us to withdraw from the whole world. They wouldn't want that for us. Life goes on around us. It's okay to feel the pain. To be sad. But we should still grab hold of things that bring us joy."

"And you seem to enjoy spending time with Ethan, don't you?" Violet added.

"I do. He's a good friend. But I don't think it would be fair to him to go out with him. I'm… I'm still in love with John."

"And that doesn't ever have to change," Rose said softly. "But you can still have feelings for someone else. You could at least go out with him and see how it goes. See how you feel about him then."

"I could, but what if I mess up our friendship? What if… what if I find out that I can't have feelings like that… like love… for someone else besides John?"

"I think it's okay to not know how it's going to work out. And maybe you will want to just remain friends. Maybe that's what you need. But I don't think it would hurt to try one date." Rose gently tapped her fingers on the arm of her chair. "And you should talk to Ethan about how you feel. Tell him what you just told us. So both of you go on the date with your eyes open."

"Listen to Rose. She gives sage advice." Violet picked up her cup and took a sip of coffee, watching Melody over the rim of her cup. So, Ethan had finally, finally asked her out. She hid a smile. She bet Melody would say yes to him after she had a bit of time to get used to the idea. Seemed like all of her friends and family were finding someone and falling in love. Rob, Collette, and now maybe Melody would find happiness with Ethan.

She loved that everyone was finding happiness, but a tiny part inside of her twinged, wondering what that would feel like. Wondering if she'd ever find someone to fall in love with. Someone to share her life with. But she had a mighty fine life now, she reminded herself. She didn't really need anything more.

Tara worked the morning crowd at Jimmy's, slipping into the familiar routine and letting it keep her from concentrating on Lance. Thinking about him. Wondering about him. At least she'd get to see him soon at the picnic. She'd thankfully already picked out what she was wearing, and she swore it was the right choice. Cute shorts and top, because she planned on playing the volleyball and horseshoes that Brandy hated so much.

But what to wear to the reunion tonight? That was another matter.

"Whatcha thinking about?" Aspen walked up and set down a tray of dirty dishes.

"You caught me. I was trying to figure out what to wear to the reunion."

"Oh, how about we sneak away for a quick shopping trip? Margaret was in and told me she got in a new shipment of cute clothes. Let's run over there. Walker won't mind."

"I won't mind what?" Walker came up behind them.

"We want to go shopping for an outfit for Tara to wear tonight."

"Really? Tara said she'd go shopping? Her closet definitely needs an upgrade. She never shops for clothes."

"I do, too." Though really it had been forever.

"By all means, go. Have fun. Maybe she'll even buy more than one outfit."

She glared at him. "I just need something to wear tonight. And my closet is fine. Lots of perfect clothes." Not really, but she didn't want to give him the satisfaction of agreeing with him.

"I'll be back soon." Aspen gave Walker a quick kiss on the cheek.

They hurried out of Jimmy's, down the wharf, and into town to Barbara's Boutique. It was now owned by Margaret, but the name had never changed through multiple changes of ownership.

Margaret greeted them as they came in. "Hello, ladies. Did you decide to do some shopping after I told you about the new shipment, Aspen?"

"No, we're here for a dress for Tara to wear to the reunion tonight."

"Oh, there are some really cute ones that came in. Come, I'll show you."

They followed Margaret to the rack of dresses, and Tara sorted through them, uncertain. One was too low-cut. One was a

RESTAURANT ON THE WHARF

lousy shade for her. Another one just wasn't her style. "I don't know." She sighed.

"How about this one?" Aspen pulled out a simple yellow dress—not quite sundress, not quite dressy dress—with a bit of fancy white stitching along the bottom.

"Go try it on," Margaret suggested.

She went into the dressing room and slipped on the dress, turning this way and that. She did like it. And it was her favorite color. Fancier than most things in her closet, but in an understated way. She actually loved it. Perfect for an outside event.

She went out to show Aspen and Margaret. Aspen clapped her hands in delight. "That looks wonderful on you."

"It really does look like it was made for you," Margaret agreed.

"I have some dressy flats that I think will work with it."

"No heels?" Aspen asked.

"No, I'm not going to take a chance on breaking my ankle." She laughed. "I'm afraid I'm just not a heel person."

She looked at the tag, pleasantly surprised it wasn't too pricey. But then Margaret was known for finding nice clothes at an affordable price. She bought the dress, and they walked outside into the sunshine.

"I'd better hurry back to Jimmy's." Aspen held a hand up to block the sun from her eyes. "But I love the dress you picked out."

"I'll take this home and change for the picnic. I really appreciate you going shopping with me."

"Walker will be pleased we had success."

"Right, but ask him the last time *he* went shopping." She shook her head.

Aspen laughed. "He said he had one kind of pants he liked and always ordered them online when he wore out a pair. And his shorts he picks up at that shop on the wharf."

"And he wears his Jimmy's on the Wharf shirts everywhere." She grinned. "So he's one to talk about upgrading a closet."

Aspen gave her a quick hug. "Have fun at the picnic, and I'll still be over this evening to help with your hair. Might as well get some use out of that time I worked at the hair salon. I mean, I didn't actually do hair. I ran the reception desk, answered the phone, and swept floors, but I learned a lot. I'm pretty good with a flatiron."

"And I appreciate the help. I'm hopeless with my hair. I'll see you then."

Aspen hurried away, and Tara turned to head home. Just enough time left to get ready for the picnic so she didn't end up wearing her Jimmy's t-shirt like she'd just accused Walker of doing all the time.

CHAPTER 21

Lance never showed up for the picnic, and Tara did her best to hide her disappointment. Joey saw through her, though. She could tell. But he kept his comments to himself.

The good thing was, Brandy didn't show up either. Although that might have meant Brandy was off with Lance. But that didn't bother her. Really, it didn't.

Joey went to grab them both a beer, and they sat in the shade of a live oak. She pressed the cold can against her forehead. "Got hot out there playing volleyball."

"It did. I don't remember you being so competitive in high school."

"I just needed to blow off some steam." Because it bothered her that Lance hadn't shown up. *And* it bothered her that it bothered her. She rolled her eyes at herself. What a case she was.

She needed to just get over Lance. He obviously wasn't interested. He'd probably hooked back up with Brandy. And Brandy was his type. Beautiful, vivacious, and ran in the same circles that Lance did. He didn't want to go out with someone who worked in a restaurant. She wasn't even in his league.

She hated this twisted knot in her stomach and the way her emotions rumbled over her like a steamroller.

"Penny for your thoughts." Joey leaned against the tree.

"You don't want to know." She shook her head.

"Thinking about Lance?" He gave her a knowing look. Of course, he knew what she was thinking.

"I was. And don't you think after all this time I could just get over him?"

"Our heart doesn't always listen to our head."

But was it really her heart? Did she have real feelings for Lance, or was it still just some silly schoolgirl crush? And wasn't she old enough to be over that? Besides, Lance had been hot and cold with her this week. The whole situation irked her.

And why had he kissed her? It had only made things worse.

"Well, I'm too old for this nonsense. He's obviously not interested in me."

Joey didn't look one bit upset with her comment. Figures. Joey never was much of a fan of Lance's.

"So, want me to come over and we'll go to the reunion together tonight?"

"You don't have to do that."

"What if I want to?" He nudged her with his shoulder.

"Who am I to deny you what you want?" She grinned, enjoying his companionship. Enjoying how uncomplicated it was being with Joey.

"So, after that beer, you want to take on the champions in the horseshoe tournament? You were always good at horseshoes." Joey cocked his head. "You know, just so you can let loose your competitive streak." He winked at her. "I mean, let off some steam."

"Yes, let's go show them how it's done." She stood.

Joey popped up. "Atta girl. That's the attitude."

They headed over to horseshoes, which she was sure would take her mind off Lance. Positive.

Pretty certain.

Tara stood in her robe, freshly showered, and stared in the mirror at her impossible hair. "You sure you can do something with this? I guess I could always wear it up in a bun."

Aspen pushed her into a chair. "Sit. Trust me. I can do this." Aspen took some hair products out of her bag, one after the other, and went to work.

She watched in the mirror as Aspen skillfully used the blow dryer to dry her hair. Then worked some magic with the flatiron to straighten her hair a bit. Then she watched in amazement as Aspen put *perfect* beach waves into her hair. A bit of hair spray, but not too much, and her hair was transformed.

"Wow, I can't believe it." She reached up and touched her hair, glad to see that it didn't feel stiff or sticky.

"Looks great. Let's do your makeup now."

"I was just going to use a bit of mascara and some lip gloss."

Aspen shook her head and grinned at her. "Not tonight." She pulled out a cosmetic case.

"I don't like a lot of makeup," she protested.

"Don't worry. I won't overdo it. Trust me."

Aspen put a light foundation, a touch of eyeshadow, and a hint of blush on her. Tara put on her own mascara, and Aspen handed her an eyelash curler. "Here, use this."

When she was finished, she looked in the mirror, amazed at how she looked. Her hair drifted around her shoulders in lovely waves. Her makeup made her face look radiant but not overdone.

She stood up and gave Aspen a hug. "You are a wizard at this."

Aspen laughed. "I've learned a few tricks along the way." Aspen gave her a gentle push.

"Now go put on the dress and don't mess up your hair."

She put on the dress they'd found this afternoon, then slipped on her shoes. Walking over to the full-length mirror, she stared at her reflection. She looked like herself... only different. She looked more put together.

She twirled around to face Aspen. "I can't thank you enough."

"You look beautiful." Aspen picked up her things and stashed them back in her bag. "Of course, I always think you look beautiful. You just look... I don't know... fancier tonight."

"I feel like Cinderella." She laughed and twirled around in front of the mirror again. The dress swished around her in a soft circle.

"Okay, I'm going to duck out now. I told Walker I'd be back to help out at Jimmy's. He said to tell you to have fun. And I can't wait to hear all about it tomorrow. Don't forget any details."

"I won't." She walked Aspen to the door and opened it. Joey stood in the doorway, his hand raised for a knock. His eyes lit up in appreciation. "Wow, Tara, you look stunning."

Her heart pounded at the compliment.

"Thanks, Joey. You look pretty good yourself."
He was dressed in a tan suit and a white shirt.
The perfect suit for a fancy beach event.
Though she bet *he* didn't spend hours getting
ready.

CHAPTER 22

Aspen slipped past him and smiled. "You two have a great time tonight."

"Thanks, Aspen," Joey said without taking his eyes off Tara. "You really do look great, Tara. The yellow looks great on you."

"Great. There's that word again."

He grinned. "I told you it was one of my favorite words."

"Obviously." She shook her head, and the loose curls drifted across her shoulders.

He'd never seen her hair like that. It was pretty, but he wasn't sure he didn't like it better when it was free and full of curls and a bit wild. "I drove over instead of walking. I wasn't sure if you'd have heels on or what."

She looked down at her shoes. "Nope, just flats. But driving sounds good."

They walked to his car, and he opened the passenger door for her. She slid inside, her long legs flashing briefly before she folded them into the car.

He walked around to his side and got inside. A tension crackled through the car, but he was pretty sure he was the only one feeling it. Though Tara's eyes did shine with excitement. Unfortunately, that excitement was for seeing Lance, he reminded himself. Then reminded himself again.

After the short drive to The Cabot Hotel, he pulled up to the valet parking and gave them his keys. "You here for the reunion, sir?"

"I am."

"Just head through the lobby, then on back outside toward the bay. The pavilion is back that way."

Tara took his arm, and he smiled to himself. At least he had her now. They could share going to the reunion, at least. As they headed through the lobby, he could tell she was a bit nervous. Most likely anxious about seeing Lance again. They went outside and entered the pavilion.

White lights were strung around the edge, and a small band sat at the far end with a dance floor spilling out in front of them. Tables were scattered around, and the serving tables were set up, just waiting for the buffet food to be brought out.

"Oh, it looks lovely, doesn't it?" Her eyes lit up as sparkly as the lights.

"I was going to say it looks great." He grinned and was rewarded with her answering laugh.

They took a few steps in, and she started to scan the crowd and then her breath caught. He glanced toward where she was looking, and there he was. Lance. His heart plummeted even while he told himself that was silly. Of course she was looking for Lance. She liked him. Had a thing for him.

He snagged two glasses of champagne from a passing server. "Come on, let's go mingle."

He led the way through the crowd and over toward Lance, even though that was the last place he wanted to be. As they approached, Lance broke into a wide smile. "Tara, you look fabulous tonight."

She looked fabulous all the time, but he didn't correct Lance.

Tara blushed and dropped her hand from his arm. The spot she deserted turned instantly cool and abandoned.

"Hi, Lance. We missed you at the picnic today." He tried to sound friendly.

"Got tied up with my dad. Sorry to miss it." He didn't really sound sorry, though. "Hey, Duffy, you don't mind if I steal Tara, do you? How about a dance, Tara?"

"I'd love to."

"Duffy, take her drink," Lance commanded more than asked.

Tara looked at him, and he nodded, taking her champagne. Lance led her out onto the dance floor, and he felt instantly alone. But he should be happy, right? Tara was getting what she wanted. A dance with Lance. He just better treat her right, or Lance would have to answer to him.

But Tara practically glowed with happiness out there on the dance floor with Lance. He was happy for her. He was. Just like a good friend should be.

Only his heart was crumbling into tiny, jagged pieces, tearing him apart.

It's what Tara wants and you're happy for her. He repeated it over and over again like a mantra, but it didn't seem to help one bit.

He looked down at the two glasses of champagne in his hands and took a sip of his. It was going to be a very long night watching Tara and Lance.

CHAPTER 23

Tara had taken Lance's offered hand and walked out onto the dance floor, her heart pounding in her chest. She knew she had a silly grin on her face that she tried to hide. He twirled her around once and laughed. "Looking good there, Bodine."

They danced to a few fast songs she remembered from high school, then the music changed to a slow song. Lance took her into his arms and pulled her close. "Ah, finally," he said.

Did he say that? Did she really hear him say 'ah, finally'? Her heart tripped in her chest and her pulse raced.

"Come on, Tara, relax."

She tried, she really did. She leaned closer,

moving slowly to the music, enjoying every single moment and every single movement. Here she was, dancing a slow dance with Lance. Hadn't that been her dream for years? And hadn't his eyes lit up when he saw her tonight? Maybe the hot and cold wavering attitude was over. He sure was acting like he was interested in her tonight.

She looked over toward the edge of the dance floor and saw Brandy standing there glaring at her with a you're-not-good-enough look. Luckily, Lance turned slightly, taking her with him and blocking Brandy from her view. She didn't want anything to interfere with this moment.

They danced a few more dances, then Lance snagged them champagne, and they walked over to the edge of the pavilion. The cool breeze blew her curls, and she hoped they weren't working themselves into a disaster.

Lance lounged against the railing and watched the crowd for a bit. "It's not as bad as I thought. At least they had the reunion at The Cabot. It's really the only nice place in town."

She didn't agree that it was the only place, but she didn't want to correct him.

"You should see my suite. It's really nice. I got the top-floor suite with a balcony. Mr. Hamilton did a good job on the remodel. Of course, he is a Hamilton, and Hamilton Hotels are known for their quality. I often stay at them on business trips." He took a sip of his champagne. "Say, would you like to see the suite? I mean, I guess you'd never have a reason to reserve the suite for yourself since you live here in town, but it is really nice. Has a nice view. We could go see the view and catch the breeze up there."

"I… uh… sure." She *was* curious to see how it looked. And it would be nice to get away from the noise for a bit. She looked around to tell Joey where she was going but couldn't see him. Oh, well, she wouldn't be gone long.

"Come on." Lance took her arm and led her out of the pavilion. They walked back into the hotel and took the elevator to the top floor. "You're going to love this," he said as he unlocked the door, stepped inside, and flipped on a low lamplight.

She followed him into the suite and swept her gaze in awe. The room was gorgeous. Well decorated, but so tastefully done. The double doors to the bedroom were open to the right. The main room held a white leather sofa, two chairs, and a table. A small kitchen was tucked off the other side of the room. A full bar graced one corner. The far side of the room was covered in full-length windows and a French door leading out to the balcony. It was truly outstanding. She'd have to tell Mr. Hamilton how lovely it was the next time he came into Jimmy's.

"Come see the view." Lance walked over and threw open the doors. She stepped out and took in the sight.

The pavilion was lit up down near the bay. She could see the lights from a few boats out in the harbor. All the walkways around the hotel were lit up with low lights lining the sidewalks. Stars twinkled above, and a slice of moon reflected on the harbor. "It's just beautiful."

"Yeah, best view in town." He took her elbow. "But let's go back inside. It's muggy out here."

She thought it was perfect out here and would have loved to stay and just soak in that view. But he was right. They should get back to the reunion.

They walked back inside, and he closed the French door behind him. He paused, and she bumped into him. He turned back around and placed one hand on each side of the closed French door behind her, leaning close. She swallowed, feeling the cool door against her back. He bent his head and kissed her, deepening the kiss until it was hard and demanding. A real kiss. But...

She pushed at his chest. "Ah, Lance." She ducked under his arm and took a few steps, not missing the gleam in his eyes.

"Oh, come on. Don't play hard to get. I know you've had a crush on me since we were kids."

She whirled around to hide the deep blush clinging to her cheeks. He knew that? That she'd had a crush on him?

He took a step forward, and she felt the heat of him behind her. He put a hand on her shoulder. "You know you've wanted this for years." He kissed her shoulder and turned her around to face him.

He kissed her again, demanding, his hands clenching her shoulders tightly. But there were no fireworks, no surge of passion, no...

anything. She pulled back. This was not what she wanted. What she had thought she had always wanted. "No, Lance. I just wanted to see the suite. Nothing more."

"Come on, don't be like that. You know you want to sleep with me. It will be fun." He threw her his boyish grin. One that probably always got him anything he wanted. But not this time.

Her eyes widened. "You thought I wanted to *sleep* with you? I hardly know you."

"What do you mean? You've known me for years."

"But... not like that. Not like a boyfriend or something." Her words jumbled in her head. "No, Lance. I don't want this. I mean, yes, I did have a crush on you back then. And when you asked me out, I thought I was finally having the wish come true. That you'd notice me and ask me on a date."

"And I did, didn't I?" He took a step forward again.

She stepped back and ran into a chair. He stood there—looking taller and bigger than she remembered. His eyes glinted with desire. Her pulse raced as she glanced over and gauged the distance to the door. "You did ask me out. But...

this isn't what I want. You don't really want me. You want... a conquest. You don't care about me."

He frowned, shaking his head. "Why are you making this so complicated?"

"It's *not* complicated, Lance. I don't want to sleep with you."

He stepped forward quickly, a coaxing smile replacing his frown. "Of course you do." He leaned forward, grabbing her shoulders firmly, and kissed her again.

She shoved against his hard chest and pulled back, then drew back her hand and slapped him with all the force she could muster. "I'm leaving." She stared down at her hand for a split second, stinging from the impact.

"Come on, Tara. Don't be like that." He stretched out his hand toward her, but she slipped out of his reach.

She whirled around and fled out of the suite, wondering how she could have been so stupid. Why had she gone up to his suite? Just to see it. Ha. How naive was she? How foolish? She wasn't some silly teen now. She was a grown woman who should have known better.

But how had he thought she'd sleep with him? Was he crazy?

No, she was crazy. For ever thinking he was something special. For ever having a crush on him.

She glanced behind to make sure he wasn't following her, then pushed into the stairwell and fled down the stairs. Tears started to fall, and she slashed her hand across her cheek, wiping them away. Humiliation and anger swirled through her.

She was so very, very foolish.

CHAPTER 24

Joey saw Tara walk back into the pavilion, her face flushed. And maybe he was crazy, but he'd swear she'd been crying. He hurried across the distance, worry surging through him. "You okay?"

"I'm fine. Never been better." She was lying. That much was obvious.

"You sure?"

"I said I was, didn't I?" she snapped.

"Okay." He held up two hands knowing full well she wasn't fine.

"I'm sorry. Didn't mean to be rude."

"How about a drink, then?" He watched her carefully.

"I'd love one. The coldest beer you can find. No more champagne."

He kept his eye on her while he went and got them both a beer and returned quickly to her side. She grabbed the beer from him and took a long swallow, then another. Then she swiped her hand across her lips as if she were scrubbing them.

"You want to talk?" he asked softly, trying one more time, certain something was wrong. And just as certain that it involved Lance.

"Nope." She took another swallow of beer and tossed her head, her hair flying in all directions and the carefully done waves twisting into the wild curls he loved so much.

In the distance, he saw Brandy sidle up to Lance as he walked into the pavilion. She placed her hand on Lance's arm as if she owned him. Joey glanced over at Tara to see if she was catching this and how she would take it.

Tara didn't take her eyes off them.

Lance leaned down and said something to Brandy. She nodded, smiled, and flipped her hair in that annoying way she'd always had. Lance put his arm around her shoulder and they head out of the pavilion.

"Looks like Lance is going to get his conquest tonight, after all." Tara took another sip of her beer, her voice icy cold.

He narrowed his eyes and stared at Tara. "What are you talking about?"

"Lance and Brandy."

He looked at her closely. "What happened? Are you sure you're okay?"

"I'm fine. I told you." She grabbed his hand. "Come on. Let's dance."

He followed her out to the dance floor, and they danced until he could hardly move. Song after song. Hits from when they were growing up. Finally, thankfully, they put on a slow song. "You up for this?"

She nodded. He wrapped his arm around her waist and took her hand in his. They slowly swayed to the music, and he began to catch his breath. She leaned her forehead against his chest, and he could swear he heard her gulp back tears. He wasn't sure what was wrong exactly, but he was fairly certain it involved Lance. It was obvious she didn't want to talk about it now, but maybe she would later.

The reunion finally wound down—with no

sign of Lance or Brandy returning—and Tara turned to him. "You ready to go?"

"Sure. Whenever you are."

He led her out to the car, and they drove back to her apartment in silence. He walked her to her door, wondering if he should ask what was wrong once again. But the look on her face said he should back off. Then he saw a tear slipping down her cheek and gave up.

"Ah, Tara. It's Lance, isn't it?"

She nodded as the tears began to run down her cheeks.

He pulled her into his arms and let her cry. She grabbed hold of him as sobs racked through her and her tears drenched his shirt. He stroked her back, trying to keep his anger in check. Lance was no good. Never had been. And now he'd hurt Tara. He'd never forgive him for that.

She finally stopped crying—mostly—and stepped back. "I'm sorry."

"Don't be sorry." He looked at her swollen, red eyes and his heart tore into pieces. If only he could have prevented her pain. He shouldn't have encouraged her with Lance. He should have done everything in his power to keep her away from him. The man was bad news.

"Want to talk about it?"

"No, I just need time to sort it all out."

"Whatever you need." He would always give her whatever she needed.

"I... I should go in." She turned to unlock the door.

He reached out and touched her arm. "Hey, there's one more thing I'd like to do before I leave."

She turned back to face him. "What's that?"

"I'd like to go over to Belle Island. Go to Magic Cafe. Go to Lighthouse Point. Will you come with me tomorrow?"

"Sure. That sounds like fun." But her eyes didn't light up like they usually did when she had the opportunity to go to the beach. "Can we go in the afternoon? I'm beat."

"Sure. I'll pick you up at one?"

She nodded and slipped inside without another word.

He trudged back to his car, certain something had happened. Maybe she'd talk tomorrow when they went to Lighthouse Point.

It had always been a magical place for them. Seemed fitting that it would be where he'd spend his last day with Tara. He was headed back to California on Monday morning, a thought that held no appeal whatsoever.

CHAPTER 25

On Sunday morning, Melody kept glancing up when the cafe door opened. Ethan hadn't been in since they talked on Friday. That wasn't like him. He was usually in once every day, if not twice. She didn't really blame him for avoiding her, though. But then, maybe he was just giving her space. Wasn't he giving her what she needed? What she asked for? She did say she needed time to think things over.

And she was thinking it over.

And overthinking it.

After talking to Rose and Violet, the date had started to sound like not such a bad idea after all. But Rose was right. She needed to talk to Ethan first. Explain things. Then he could choose whether to go out with her or not. He'd have to know she still loved John and always would. But did that mean she could never love another man? That was the question she had no answer for.

Her breath caught when he finally came in and took a seat. She hurried over to where Evelyn was putting a fresh batch of ice cream behind the ice cream counter. "Hey, Evelyn. I need a few minutes. That okay?"

Evelyn glanced over to where Ethan was sitting, a small smile on her lips. "Sure, I'll tell Livy to cover for you. Take all the time you need."

"I really need to talk to him for a few minutes."

"Then go, talk." Evelyn shooed her away, still smiling.

She walked over to Ethan's table and he glanced up, a tentative look on his face. "Good morning, Melody."

"Can we talk?"

He nodded, and she sank onto the seat

across from him. "I've been thinking about what you asked. About me going on a date with you."

He sat there silently, looking like he was waiting for terrible news. He clutched his coffee mug with both hands.

She took a deep breath. "The date... it's not totally a bad idea."

A small smile lifted the corners of his mouth, and he released the mug.

"But you have to know something. Understand it."

His forehead creased, and he nodded.

"I'm... I'm still in love with John. I always will be. I miss him every single day. It hurts my heart." She reached across the table and took his hand. "But a wise person told me I can't hide away the rest of my life. And she's right. I've just been going through the motions of living since John died. Trying to fill my days. But I think... I think I'd like to go out on a date with you. I don't know how it will work out, but we could try it. If you still want to after hearing all that."

"I'd like that very much." He covered her hand with his. "And that's okay that you love

John. I'd never try to take that away from you. Never try to replace that love."

The knot in her stomach loosened with his understanding, with his words. "But you have to promise me if this dating thing doesn't work out, that we'll still be friends. I couldn't bear to lose you as a friend."

"Then I promise, we'll still be friends. No matter what." His eyes shone with honesty and hopefulness. "We'll work it out."

"Then I say yes. Yes, I'll go out on a date with you. Maybe something simple? A dinner out or something like that?"

"I'd love to take you out to dinner."

Her heart tripped a bit, but she was sure she was making the right decision. And what better person than Ethan to go out with on her first date after John? Ethan was kind, and patient, and easy to talk to. And she cared about him. Who knew where things could lead?

Ethan's eyes lit up and his lips spread into a wide grin. "We'll have a great time. You'll see." Then his eyes narrowed a bit. "But at any time, if you change your mind, if it's too much for you, you just let me know."

"I will." Relief bubbled through her. She'd

talked to him. Made her decision to go out with him. And it felt very right. "I need to get back to work. But I'm glad you came in."

"I am, too. Really glad."

She stood and headed back to the kitchen, with one quick glance back at Ethan, who sat at the table with a huge grin. She smiled. Yes, if she was ever going to try dating again, Ethan was the perfect man.

She pushed into the kitchen and Evelyn looked up. "Well, did you talk to him?"

"I did."

"And?" Evelyn put down the dish towel and walked over to her.

"And… I'm going on a date with him."

Evelyn's eyes lit up, and she hugged her. "It's about time."

"What do you mean?" She stepped back and stared at Evelyn.

"Honey, that man has been head over heels for you forever."

She glanced back at the doorway to the cafe. "He has?"

"Yes, he has. And you were the only one who didn't see it." Evelyn took her hand and squeezed it. "But maybe you weren't ready to see it. And now you are. Maybe now is the right time."

"Maybe it is." She nodded as a small smile tugged at the corners of her mouth. Maybe it was the perfect time.

CHAPTER 26

Tara woke up early, even though she was still exhausted. Her mind could not turn off. Flashes of last night danced through her mind. She could still feel Lance's powerful grip on her shoulders and noticed bruises there when she got dressed. She put on a t-shirt to cover them.

She was such a foolish woman. What had she been thinking when she said she'd go up to his room? Well, she knew what *she'd* been thinking. She wanted to see what the suite was like and see the view. Definitely not what Lance had in mind.

She tugged on her shoes and headed over to

see if her mom was home. Sometimes a woman just needed her mom.

She walked in the door to her parents' house and called out. "Mom? You home?"

"Back in the kitchen."

She headed to the kitchen where her mom was unloading the dishwasher. "There's still some coffee." Her mom nodded toward the coffeemaker.

"Thanks." She grabbed a familiar mug and poured herself some coffee before sinking into a kitchen chair.

Her mother put away the last dish, refilled her cup, and sat down beside her. "So, did you have a good time at the reunion?"

"I... no." She ran her hand through her now wild curls. "Well, yes, with Joey."

"You might need to explain a bit better." Her mother gave her a gentle smile.

"Well, Lance was there, too." She sighed and leaned back in her chair.

"I know you always had a thing for Lance in high school. And you were excited to go out with him this week."

"Right, about that." She set her cup down and leaned her elbows on the table. "Oh, Mom, he's not the man I thought he was. At all." She closed her eyes against the memories of being in his suite last night.

"People can change a lot in twenty-five years."

She opened her eyes and stared at her mother's face. When had her mother gotten older? She always pictured her mother as younger in her mind. But Mom had her fair share of wrinkles now, and her hair was totally gray. But the face was the same. Kind, always a smile. So good to talk to. Always willing to listen.

"I hope… I hope I never see Lance again."

"Oh, honey. I'm sorry." Her mother's eyes filled with sympathy.

"Maybe I didn't know him back then. Maybe he's always been like this."

"Maybe." Her mother squeezed her hand. "But Joey hasn't changed, has he? He's still that sweet, kind boy he was all those years ago."

"Yes, Joey's the same. I can always depend on Joey."

"And…" Her mother paused and looked deeply into her eyes. "And he's still in love with you."

"What? Joey doesn't love me. We're friends." She sat back in her chair, amazed at her mother's statement. They were *friends*.

Her mother gave a gentle laugh. "Yes, you're friends. But Joey wants more. He always has."

"It's not like that between us."

"Isn't it? How do you feel about him?"

"I feel like he's my best friend. Someone I can talk to about anything. Someone who understands me. I love him… but I'm not *in* love with him." She frowned. And yet, when she thought about him leaving, didn't it tear her heart into shreds? Could she really imagine a day here in Moonbeam without him after this last week?

His easy smile when he saw her. His teasing. The fun time they had romping in the gulf like kids. The way he'd held her when she cried about Lance.

Had she fallen in love with Joey Duffy?

Her mouth dropped open, and she set her cup down with a clatter. "Mom, did anyone ever tell you that you're the smartest woman in the world?"

Her mother's eyes twinkled. "Can't say that they have."

She jumped up and hugged her mother. "I have to go find Joey."

Her mother smiled. "I thought maybe you did."

Joey looked up as he walked out of Sea Glass Cafe after a wonderful breakfast. And there was Lance, standing right on the sidewalk. The last person he wanted to see. He balled his fists and took three quick steps up to him. "Lance."

"Duffy." Lance cocked his head.

"What happened last night?" Joey growled the words.

"What are you talking about?" Lance feigned innocence.

"What happened between you and Tara?"

"Hey, not that it's any of your business, but she went up with me to my suite. What do you think we did?" Lance rolled his eyes. "What does any man do with a woman in his suite?"

His breath caught. Tara went up to Lance's suite?

"I showed her a real good time." Lance winked.

Tara had slept with Lance? Anger and hurt surged through him. But then, why had Tara been so upset? Crying?

"Lance, you're an idiot."

"Pretty sure that's not what Tara thinks." Lance laughed, turned away, and strode down the sidewalk.

Joey leaned against the brick wall of Parker's. That's what Tara was crying about? Because she slept with Lance? How could she do that? Sleep with him?

But hadn't she always had a crush on him? Wasn't that always what she wanted? For Lance to notice her? He clenched his teeth. Evidently, Lance had noticed *all* of her last night.

That still didn't explain the tears.

But then Lance had headed out with Brandy on his arm. Maybe *that's* what upset Tara. Maybe Lance had a *double-dip* last night.

Anger swept through him. Anger at Lance. Anger at Tara. Anger at himself for being so foolish about Tara. It would never change. She'd always have a thing for Lance. Always.

It was a good thing he was leaving tomorrow, but he couldn't keep doing this. Supporting her when she kept going after

Lance, then propping her up when he disappointed her.

He was a fool.

He contemplated calling and cancelling their trip to Belle Island. But a tiny part of him couldn't leave without saying goodbye to her. Seeing her one last time. And this was the last time he was ever coming back to Moonbeam. The very last time. He'd learned his lesson well.

He'd go to Belle Island with her. Go to Magic Cafe and see Tally. Have one last trip to Lighthouse Point. And he knew what his wish would be at Lighthouse Point. He'd wish to get Tara totally out of his system. Out of his thoughts. He'd wish to not feel a single twinge of emotion about her.

If he did all that, he will have checked off everything he'd wanted to do on this trip.

Well, except one *big* thing. The thing that would never happen now.

CHAPTER 27

Tara raced back to her apartment and put on a sundress and sandals. There was no helping her hair, so she just pulled it back in a ponytail. She wished she had some of Aspen's makeup and made a mental note to go shopping for some. Mascara and lip gloss would have to do for today.

Her cheeks had a rosy glow about them now, though. And she knew why and it wasn't from makeup.

She threw open the door when Joey knocked, a goofy grin on her face. "There you are, right on time."

He glanced at his watch. "Yep, on time. You ready?"

No look of appreciation in his eyes. No special smile. She frowned. "You okay?"

"Me? Of course."

She stepped outside and followed him over to his car. He held her door open, and she slipped inside, a bit nervous to talk to him. Maybe she'd wait until they got to Magic Cafe. A familiar place. One where they'd had lots of good times. Yes, Magic Cafe would be perfect.

He climbed inside, started the engine, and pulled out of the drive. He barely said a word on their trip to Belle Island, and that wasn't like him.

"You excited to see the island again?" she asked.

"Yeah, sure." Not much enthusiasm. This wasn't like Joey.

"And Magic Cafe. You love their grouper." She laughed. "Of course, you love any kind of grouper."

"Uh-huh."

This was harder than she expected. She glanced over at him and noticed a sharpness to his features. What was wrong with him? Last night he'd been so sweet and understanding.

Now it was like… it was like he didn't want to be here. To be with her.

Maybe her mother had been wrong…

Had she? Because Joey sure wasn't a man who was acting like he cared about her. That he wanted to be with her.

He pulled into the crushed shell drive of Magic Cafe and came around and opened her car door. The perfect gentleman.

And nothing more.

She followed him inside the restaurant and they cut through to the outdoor seating.

"Joey Duffy." Tally smothered him in a hug. "Look at you. All grown up."

"Tally, good to see you." Joey's lips curled into the first smile she'd seen from him all day.

"And Tara. Welcome. You two haven't been here together since you were kids. Come, let me give you a beachside table."

They sat down across from each other, and Joey stared out at the beach, out at the waves.

"Everything is still the same, isn't it?"

Joey turned back to her. "No, not everything."

"Really? What's changed here?" She swept her gaze around the restaurant.

"You, Tara. You've changed."

She frowned. "Some. I mean, I'm older now. But I'm still the same person."

"Are you?" His eyes glittered with… was that anger?

Was Joey *mad* at her?

"Joey, what's wrong?"

"Nothing."

But he was lying.

They ordered their meal, and he hardly said anything. One-word answers to her questions, though he was perfectly friendly with Tally when she came by their table to check on them.

Finally, she'd had enough. "Joey Duffy. Tell me what's wrong. And don't say nothing, because you'd be lying."

He looked over at her with a look full of… disapproval?

He leaned forward, glaring at her. "Okay, I'll tell you. I'll tell you what's wrong. I ran into Lance in town this morning."

"Oh?"

"Yes, and he told me what happened last night."

Now that surprised her. Why would Lance

tell Joey that he didn't score with her? That she'd turned him down. Slapped him.

"I didn't think he'd say anything to anyone." She shook her head.

"Well, you know how he is. He likes to boast about his conquests."

A frown creased her brow, and she stared at Joey. "His conquests? What are you talking about?"

"You, Tara. How you slept with him? I mean, you hardly know him. Just because you had a schoolgirl crush on him years ago, do you think that's a good reason to sleep with him now? But then, you do you." He pushed back from a table and crossed his arms, anger flashing in his eyes. "You're a grown woman capable of making your own decisions. Isn't that what you're always saying?" His eyes had turned to an icy blue, and he held his lips in a straight, firm line.

Her mouth dropped open. "I don't know what Lance told you. But I did *not* sleep with him."

"But he said—"

She held up her hand, cutting him off. "I can't believe you thought I would *sleep* with him.

You know me better than that. I don't care what he said to you."

"But he said you went up to his suite."

"That I did. And it was foolish on my part. He said he had the fancy top-floor suite and a wonderful view. I wanted to see it. You know, see how the other half lives. The kind that can afford fancy things like that." She shook her head. "But I didn't sleep with him. He wanted me to... he didn't really want to take no for an answer." She reached up and touched her shoulder, remembering.

Joey's eyes narrowed, and his hand snapped across the table, reaching for her hand. "Did he hurt you?"

"Ah, no. Not really. He just surprised me and then wouldn't listen when I said I had no interest in sleeping with him. I don't think he gets turned down often. I... slapped him."

A smile crept across Joey's face. "You did? Good for you."

"So that's why you've been so quiet today? You thought I slept with Lance?"

"I was so... angry. Hurt, I guess. Though you do have the right to be with whoever you want. I just…" He shook his head. "Not Lance. The guy is not a nice guy."

"You don't have to tell me that. I'm officially over my crush on him." She grinned at Joey.

"You have no idea how pleased I am to hear that. Let's celebrate this revelation with chocolate cake." He flagged the server and ordered chocolate cake with a big scoop of vanilla ice cream.

They split the dessert, and things were finally back how they should be between them. With her friend.

Only she still had something to tell him. She just hadn't gotten up the nerve.

Joey stood. "Ready for Lighthouse Point?"

"Yes."

"Want to just walk from here?"

"I do." She nodded and followed him down the stairs and out onto the beach. He took her hand and led her to the edge of the water. The waves danced at their feet as they walked along the beach until they stood in the lighthouse's shadow.

"I love this spot." She let out a long sigh, her heart swelling with happiness. And a bit of nervousness. She needed to talk to Joey. Tell him how she felt.

"I remember." He smiled at her.

That smile of his. How could she ever have forgotten that smile of his? When he smiled at her like that, she forgot all her worries, forgot everything. "Of course you remember. You remember everything, Joey."

"Pretty much." He smiled at her again, and her breath caught in her throat and her heart pounded.

She sucked in a deep breath of air, gathering her courage. "But I think you're right. I have changed."

He turned and looked at her intently. "You have?"

"I have. I've finally realized something. Well, my mom helped me realize something."

"And what's that?"

"I love you, Joey Duffy. And not only that, I'm *in* love with you. It's just taken me years to figure out."

For once Joey stood speechless, his mouth open, until he finally broke into a wide grin. "You love me?"

"Yes. Want me to say it again?"

"Sure do."

"I love you."

"Ah, Tara. I love you, too. I have since… well, since forever." He reached out and took her into his arms, pulling her close. "And your mother is a wise, wise woman."

"She is." She tilted her head up, and he lowered his lips to hers. A thrill ran through her, a happiness so overwhelming that it filled her completely. He finally pulled away, still grinning his lazy smile that she adored.

"That was nice," she said when she finally caught her breath, then she grinned. "Dare I say it was… great?"

He laughed. "It was, wasn't it?"

"Shall we make our wishes now?" She leaned over and picked up a shell.

He paused, then grabbed one, too. She grasped the shell in her hands, made her wish, then watched as the shell sank into the sea.

She turned to him. "Hey, you didn't make a wish yet. Go ahead."

He just tossed the shell from hand to hand. "No, I don't think I will. I've already gotten the wish I made long ago. The last time we came to Lighthouse Point."

"What's that?"

"I wished for you to… like me. And not just as your best friend. Like me as a guy. Fall in love with me."

She threw her arms around him. "Well, you sure got your wish."

"You sure took your sweet time granting it," he teased.

"Am I worth the wait?" She tilted her head back to look into his eyes. The eyes shining with love.

"You are so worth the wait. You're… well… you're *great*."

She threw back her head and laughed, grabbing his hand. "Come on. Race you into the water."

"Are you crazy? We don't have our suits on."

"I don't care." She kicked off her shoes and stared at him, daring him.

Joey threw back his head and laughed as he tugged off his shirt and kicked off his shoes. He reached over and grabbed her hand. They raced into the water, splashing in the waves, kissing, laughing, and kissing some more.

They finally emerged from the water and sat

on the sand. He pushed her wet hair away from her face and kissed her. "You know what?"

"What?" She stared at his face, his sky-blue eyes, the teasing smile on his lips, searing the moment in her memory forever.

He kissed her once more. "I finally feel like I'm home."

She wrapped her arms around his neck and pulled him close. "I do, too, Joey Duffy. I do, too."

CHAPTER 28

Tara got out of the shower and grabbed her phone, looking at the text message. Her parents wanted to see her and Walker at their house. She looked at her watch and frowned. She had plans this evening with Joey. But they could swing by her parents' first.

She looked at her damp clothes, soaked in seawater and covered with sand, piled on the floor. What a fabulous time she'd had with Joey this afternoon. He was coming back here as soon as he grabbed a shower and got cleaned up, too. Her heart beat in double time just thinking about seeing him again.

She grabbed her phone and texted back that she'd be there soon.

She hurried to get dressed and decided to let her hair air-dry. Joey never complained about its wildness. It was freeing to know that she didn't have to change herself for him. Be anything she wasn't. She could just be herself and he accepted her just like that.

She went to answer the knock at the door and stood there on one foot, wrestling her sandal onto the other foot.

He leaned in and kissed her. "You look adorable."

She laughed. "You're a hopeless, romantic, lovesick man."

"I'm bewitched." He pulled her into his arms and kissed her again.

When he finally released her, she steadied herself against the door and finally got her shoe on. "Hey, my parents want me to stop by their house this evening. Do you mind?"

"Not at all."

They headed over to her parents' and as they passed by Joey's old house, the owner was standing out front and waved to them, motioning for them to come up to the porch.

"Hello there," she said.

"Phyllis, nice to see you," Tara said.

"Tara, dear. Good to see you." Phyllis turned to Joey. "And you, too, Mr. Duffy."

"Joey, please."

"So, I know you said that you didn't want to come inside the other day. Have you changed your mind?"

"I guess I haven't really thought about it." Joey swept his gaze around the front porch.

"The offer still stands. It really is a wonderful old house. George and I are sad to be leaving it."

"You're moving?" Tara hadn't heard that.

"We're moving to be closer to our grandkids. We feel like we're missing out on too many moments in their lives. Ball games, school events. We see them for the big things, but we're missing so many of the ordinary moments. We want to be there for those."

"You're selling it?" A dazed look settled on Joey's face as he stared at the house.

"We are. Going to be putting it on the market soon."

The dazed look melted into a slow grin. "You know what? I think I'd love to take you up on your offer to see the house."

"Of course. Come right in."

Tara followed them inside and wandered around the house with Joey, and Phyllis pointed out things they'd changed. They'd updated the kitchen to soft white cabinets and new appliances that brighten up the room. There was still the window seat overlooking the bay, one of Tara's favorite things about the house. A long, covered porch spread across the back of the house, overlooking the view of the bay, with ceiling fans making lazy circles on the ceiling.

Joey turned to Phyllis. "It looks really nice."

"It's going to be so hard to leave. I hope the next owner will love it as much as we do."

"Oh, I think they might." Joey's grin was the widest and brightest Tara had seen since he returned to Moonbeam. "Because when you get ready to sell, I'd love to make you an offer."

Phyllis gasped. "You would? You want to move back in here?"

"I do. It's the last place that felt like home to me. I love this house. And…" He turned to Tara, his eyes shining. "I find that I no longer have any desire to leave Moonbeam."

Tara threw her arms around him and hugged him, then jumped back quickly, warmth creeping over her face as she looked at Phyllis. "Oh, sorry."

"Don't be sorry." Phyllis smiled. "You're obviously thrilled at his news. And I can't think of a better person to have this house."

Joey gave Phyllis his contact information, and they headed across the lawn toward her parents'. She grabbed his hand and pulled him to a stop before going inside. "Are you sure?"

"I've never been so sure of anything. I'm not leaving you. I'm not leaving Moonbeam."

Her smile almost cracked her cheeks as her heart sang, and she stood on tiptoe to kiss him. "You make me incredibly happy, Joey Duffy."

"That's my most important job." He grinned back at her and pulled her into his arms, kissing her thoroughly. She just wanted to stand out here and kiss him, but she really needed to see what her parents wanted. And yet, she didn't pull away from his kisses.

"Ahem."

Tara jumped back to see her mother standing on the porch, grinning.

"Ah… Mom." A blush swept over her cheeks.

"Hi, Mrs. Bodine." Joey didn't look the least

bit nonplussed about her seeing the kiss. He turned to her. "I'll wait out here on the porch while you go in and talk with your parents."

"Nonsense, Joey," her mother said. "You come on in, too. By the looks of things—" Her gentle laugh carried over to them on the breeze. "You should probably hear this, too."

Joey took her hand, and they followed her mother into the house and back to the kitchen. Walker broke into a grin when he saw them holding hands and shot her an I-told-you-so smirk. Her mother acted like nothing had changed. That her being with Joey was the most natural thing in the world. And maybe it was.

She just stood there with the now familiar cheek-splitting grin on her face.

"You two sit." Her mother motioned to the table. "I made a peach pie. Let me get you some."

"I never say no to your pie, Mrs. Bodine." Joey settled into a chair and she sat beside him.

Her Mom brought over-generous slices of pie and cups of hot coffee. Joey took a bite. "Best pie ever."

"Thank you, Joey," her mother said.

"So, what did you want to see us about?"

Tara glanced at her parents. Her mother looked... excited? Her father looked unsure.

"Your father and I have something to tell you and Walker."

"Oh, if it's family stuff... I'll give you some privacy." Joey started to rise.

Her mother put her hand on his arm. "Don't be silly. You're family. Sit. You should hear this, too." Her mother looked over at her father. "Jimmy, why don't you tell them?"

He cleared his throat. "Your mother and I... we've made a decision. We're... we're going to retire."

"You're what?" Walker's eyes flew open in surprise and he leaned forward.

She stifled a gasp. "You're retiring?"

"Yes. We want to travel. And you two are more than capable of running the place. We're officially turning Jimmy's over to you two."

"If you want it," her mother said. "You have a choice, you know. If you want to do something else with your lives."

"I'm not leaving. I love Jimmy's." Walker looked over at her, waiting for her comment.

She wanted to say yes, but then... did she?

"Another thing you should know. Your father

has agreed that you two can make any changes you want. Make Jimmy's your own."

"I know I've fought most of your suggestions." Her father shrugged. "But most of them have been great suggestions. And it is time. It's time that you two make it what you want it to be." He shrugged again and took her mother's hand. "I'm just not big on change."

Her mother laughed. "That's an understatement if I ever heard one." She turned to Tara. "But I really do want you two to make it your own. Make sure it stays profitable and viable in today's market. Things are different from when we started it. But I know you two can make it a wonderful restaurant that will stand the test of time. Update it a bit."

Her mom looked over at her father. He nodded. "Your mother is right. I won't interfere." He paused and grinned then. "Well, I'll try not to."

"That's why he's taking me on a trip around the world."

"Really? That's something you've always wanted, Mom."

"But before we leave, we want both of you

to take some time off. Take a break. A vacation."

Walker was still staring at her. "Sis? What do you say?"

She grinned at her brother as her answer was suddenly absolutely clear to her. "Well, we're not changing the name to Walker's."

He threw back his head and laughed. "Okay, that's a deal."

"Okay, yes. Yes, this is something I'd love to do." And she knew this was the right decision for her. Jimmy's was in her blood and she loved it. And now, she could make some changes, see what it could become. Make her mark on it.

Joey squeezed her hand. "So if you're serious about Tara taking a vacation, how about I take you up north to see the fall colors? See the leaves change. We could do a long driving tour. Say two weeks?" He looked at her, then over at Walker.

"Perfect, then Aspen and I will take a vacation." Walker nodded.

"That will give me time to plan our trip." Her mother smiled. "Jimmy, this is all working out perfectly, isn't it?"

"I never could say no to you, dear. If this

makes you happy, this makes me happy." Her father leaned over and gave her mom a quick kiss on the cheek. They were still so happy after all these years.

She wanted that. She looked over at Joey. And maybe, just maybe, she'd have a chance at that.

He winked at her and nodded as if he could read her thoughts. And he probably could.

They walked out onto her parents' dock as the sun was beginning to set. Joey held her hand in his, connecting them. They sat on the chairs and watched as the clouds began to gently reach out and hug the sun.

"Wow, a lot has happened in just one day." She leaned back in her chair, still holding Joey's hand.

"It has. My wish finally came true. I found a house where I'll finally feel like I belong." He squeezed her hand. "I guess I should have asked you about buying my old house. I mean… realistically, you could end up living next to your parents, you know."

She grinned at him. "I could?"

"Yes, you could. Because I have plans for you, Tara Bodine. For us. And I don't ever plan to let you get away again. I love you. You've always held a piece of my heart."

"I guess I'm just a slow learner. Took me some time to figure out you were right there in front of me the whole time."

His lips tipped with an easy smile. "I'm glad you finally figured it out."

"I am, too."

"And you're happy with staying at Jimmy's?" His eyebrows lifted.

"I am. Before I felt like I was just Jimmy Bodine's daughter, working at the restaurant as expected. But now... now Walker and I will own it, not just work at it. We've talked about changes we'd like to make that we think will make it more profitable. But Dad, like he said, doesn't like change. But... we'll still keep it true to being Jimmy's at its core."

"I'm happy for you."

"I feel like I've finally found my place. At Jimmy's. With you." Tears of happiness crowded the corners of her eyes. Joy thrummed through her and her heart soared. "It all happened so quickly and yet I feel like it's like the last few pieces of a puzzle falling neatly into place."

"You'll always be my home," Joey said as he leaned over and kissed her gently. The sky exploded in color around them. The moment couldn't be more perfect.

CHAPTER 29

The next morning Rose looked up to see Joey jogging toward her. Oh, good, she'd have a chance to see him before he left today. She was going to miss him.

He sank onto the sand beside her. "Morning, Rose. Great sunrise, wasn't it?"

"As beautiful as always." She looked at him for a moment. He looked extremely happy for a man who was going to be leaving Moonbeam today. "Did you have a good time at the reunion?"

"I did, and I didn't."

"That's mysterious."

"Long story. But one great thing did come out of it."

"And what's that?"

"I'm staying here in Moonbeam for a while."

"You are?"

"Yep, extended my stay with Violet."

Rose laughed. "Pretty soon she's going to be filled up with long-term residents. So what made you decide to stay?"

A wide grin spread across his face. "Tara. Tara did."

"Oh?"

"Yes… you see… it appears she loves me."

Rose smiled. "And you love her, of course. I can tell by the way you talk about her."

"I do. And I've never been happier. I'm staying here in Moonbeam, and we'll figure all the rest of it out. I'll tell you one thing, though, I'm never leaving Tara again. Oh, and it appears that I'm buying a house."

"I'm so happy for you." She loved the way his eyes lit up with happiness and the grin on his face looked like it would never desert him.

He laughed and jumped up. "I'm pretty happy for myself, too. I've gotta run. Meeting Tara for breakfast. Guess I'll be seeing you lots."

He jogged up to the cottages and Rose

smiled, her heart happy for both Joey and Tara. These cottages seemed to have a bit of magic to them. People came here. Fell in love. Fell in love with Moonbeam.

She looked up at the clouds. "Did you see that, Emmett? Another happy couple."

"Just like us." She swore she heard Emmett whisper the words.

"Yes, just like us, my love."

Another book in the Blue Heron Cottages series comes to a close. Are you ready for book five, Lilacs by the Sea? You'll meet Will and Francine Winters—Frankie to her friends—celebrating their fortieth wedding anniversary at Blue Heron Cottages along with their grown daughters. But Will and Frankie are hiding a secret. Of course. There are so many secrets in Moonbeam, aren't there?

And do Melody and Ethan finally, finally get their date? And, of course, Rose makes friends with the whole Winters family. Will we ever know Rose's whole story?

I hope you've been enjoying the books.

Thanks for reading them. I appreciate all of you.

ALSO BY KAY CORRELL

COMFORT CROSSING ~ THE SERIES

The Shop on Main - Book One

The Memory Box - Book Two

The Christmas Cottage - A Holiday Novella (Book 2.5)

The Letter - Book Three

The Christmas Scarf - A Holiday Novella (Book 3.5)

The Magnolia Cafe - Book Four

The Unexpected Wedding - Book Five

The Wedding in the Grove (crossover short story between series - Josephine and Paul from The Letter.)

LIGHTHOUSE POINT ~ THE SERIES

Wish Upon a Shell - Book One

Wedding on the Beach - Book Two

Love at the Lighthouse - Book Three

Cottage near the Point - Book Four

Return to the Island - Book Five

Bungalow by the Bay - Book Six

Christmas Comes to Lighthouse Point - Book Seven

CHARMING INN ~ Return to Lighthouse Point

One Simple Wish - Book One

Two of a Kind - Book Two

Three Little Things - Book Three

Four Short Weeks - Book Four

Five Years or So - Book Five

Six Hours Away - Book Six

Charming Christmas - Book Seven

SWEET RIVER ~ THE SERIES

A Dream to Believe in - Book One

A Memory to Cherish - Book Two

A Song to Remember - Book Three

A Time to Forgive - Book Four

A Summer of Secrets - Book Five

A Moment in the Moonlight - Book Six

MOONBEAM BAY ~ THE SERIES

The Parker Women - Book One

The Parker Cafe - Book Two

A Heather Parker Original - Book Three

The Parker Family Secret - Book Four

Grace Parker's Peach Pie - Book Five

The Perks of Being a Parker - Book Six

BLUE HERON COTTAGES ~ THE SERIES

Memories of the Beach - Book One

Walks along the Shore - Book Two

Bookshop near the Coast - Book Three

Restaurant on the Wharf - Book Four

Plus more to come!

WIND CHIME BEACH ~ A stand-alone novel

INDIGO BAY ~ Save by getting Kay's complete collection of stories previously published separately in the multi-author Indigo Bay series. The three stories are all interconnected.

Sweet Days by the Bay - the collection

ABOUT THE AUTHOR

Kay Correll is a USA Today bestselling author of sweet, heartwarming stories that are a cross between women's fiction and contemporary romance. She is known for her charming small towns, quirky townsfolk, and the enduring strong friendships between the women in her books.

Kay splits her time between the Southwest coast of Florida and the Midwest of the U.S. and can often be found out and about with her camera, taking a myriad of photographs, often incorporating them into her book covers. When not lost in her writing or photography, she can be found spending time with her ever-supportive husband, knitting, or playing with her puppies - a cavalier who is too cute for his own good and a naughty but adorable Australian shepherd. Their five boys are all grown now and while she misses the rowdy boy-noise chaos, she is thoroughly enjoying her empty nest years.

Learn more about Kay and her books at kaycorrell.com

While you're there, sign up for her newsletter to hear about new releases, sales, and giveaways.

WHERE TO FIND ME:
kaycorrell.com
authorcontact@kaycorrell.com

Join my Facebook Reader Group. We have lots of fun and you'll hear about sales and new releases first!
www.facebook.com/groups/KayCorrell/

I love to hear from my readers. Feel free to contact me at authorcontact@kaycorrell.com

facebook.com/KayCorrellAuthor

instagram.com/kaycorrell

pinterest.com/kaycorrellauthor

amazon.com/author/kaycorrell

bookbub.com/authors/kay-correll

Made in the USA
Las Vegas, NV
17 May 2023

72176569R10163